Whispers from the Past

Whispers from the Past

Simone Kelly

www.urbanbooks.net

Urban Books, LLC
300 Farmingdale Road, N.Y.-Route 109
Farmingdale, NY 11735

ISBN 13: 978-1-64556-141-5
ISBN 10: 1-64556-141-0

First Trade Paperback Printing December 2020
Printed in the United States of America

10 9 8 7 6 5 4 3 2 1

*This is a work of fiction. Any references or similarities
to actual events, real people, living or dead, or to real
locales are intended to give the novel a sense of reality.
Any similarity in other names, characters, places, and
incidents is entirely coincidental.*

Distributed by Kensington Publishing Corp.
Submit Orders to:
Customer Service
400 Hahn Road
Westminster, MD 21157-4627
Phone: 1-800-733-3000
Fax: 1-800-659-2436

Dedication

I'd like to dedicate this book to Own Your Power's Writer's Lab and everyone else who has a book inside of them. Keep writing!

A book is a dream you hold in your hand.
—Neil Gaiman

Also by *Simone Kelly*

Jack of All Trades, Master of None?

At Second Glance

Like a Fly on the Wall

Acknowledgments

Thanks to my hilarious Dad, Frank Kelly, for keeping me smiling, and to Velma Gordon-Kelly, my mother's sweet spirit that watches over me. I know she is up in heaven bragging about me lol.

I'm very thankful to the team that made this happen: Lorisa Bates, who always has my back as a friend and mentor, the Urban Books family: Carl Weber, Martha Weber, Alanna Boutin, and Diane Taber-Markiewicz for polishing off my baby with their finishing touches, and my productivity coach, Sheila Hawkins of The Third Eye Group, for staying on my butt to stick to my writing deadlines!

Big shout out to the selfless people who volunteered their time by reading scenes, sharing fun story ideas, and offering feedback.:

Sharice Lamb, Ruth Fajardo, Tesha Sylvester, Monica Gonzalez, Delilah Garcia, Danielle King, Samara King, Madge King, Kim Lindstrom, Kamesha Hall, Pittershawn Palmer, Sofiyah Jones and the Cultural Expressions family, Melissa Cancio, Michelle Lee Merritiew, Jonny Merritiew, Yahzarah St. James, Valerie Crawford, Johane Rutledge, Lynn Martinez, Cherise Fisher, Charlene Brown, Wendy Sherman, Khadijah Kareem, Sheena O. Murray, Lyneise Rachelle, Warrington Etienne, Davica Williams, and Alaire Harris.

My Ride or Die Beta Readers Crew: Ayanna Cook, Keyona Saquile Lazenby, Kawanus Bailey, Cheryl Kendrick, Sophia Melendez, Sharney Moore, Mama

Acknowledgments

Jean aka Jean Finney, Ru McKenzie, Monique Nubia Sunshine, and Zya Mo.

Lastly, I want to thank YOU! I'm so grateful for you reading and sharing your support. I'll see you in the next novel. ☺

Chapter 1

Jacques

I tuned in closely to the flickering flame of the white candle and the messages flooded in. Dee sat on the other side of the table, fidgeting with the long, gold pendant that dangled from her neck. She crossed her long, caramel-colored legs and took a deep breath, bracing herself for my reply to her question.

The tension broke when my stomach gurgled from hunger. She laughed at the abrupt sound.

"I'm sorry. I missed lunch today," I explained.

Dee shook her head in disapproval. "You need to eat, Jacques. You always doing too much—"

"Wait." I held up my finger and tilted my head as the messages finally became clearer. "Are you planning on moving? I see an opportunity for you."

"Really? I have been thinking about relocating, actually. When do you think is a good time?"

"Coming up in the next nine months or so."

She leaned in, her perfume soft, yet magnetic. "Wow, really? I do need a change." She bit her bottom lip and looked into my eyes in a coquettish kind of way. "What about Miami? Can you ask your guides if that would be a good idea? Could I get a gig down here that pays as much as New York does?" Dee smiled, waiting for a reaction.

My heart sped up. Dee moving down here?

I took a deep breath, trying to get the answer, pushing back the memory of the last time we saw each other. That time we crossed the line. That time I broke my no-client rule . . . and my no-cheating rule. I tried to forget her soft lips, how she pressed her body against mine . . . her intensity. I wanted to erase the feeling of her moist mouth and the magical way she used it on me. I shook my head, trying to stay focused on her reading and keep her out of my fantasies.

I guess my face never hides what I'm feeling. Dee's brows furrowed. "What's wrong?" she asked softly.

"Oh, nothing. Just getting a lot of messages at once. Give me a moment." I pointed at her. "I'll be right back." I smiled, closed my eyes, and took a deep breath. I inhaled the sweet smell of sandalwood incense that circled us in a soft cloud.

The vision I saw was of Dee walking into calm, clear water. She was in an aqua bikini, and she looked back at me and laughed. Then she ran full speed ahead into the ocean to dive in.

I answered excitedly, "Yes, dive in. Go for it. It feels very good."

"Really? So, move? Here?" She pointed to the ground with a smirk. "Man, I really would love this weather all year 'round. I'm so sick of the snow and cold."

"I see you having at least two companies as clients. Maybe you'll be working for an agency of some kind or have several clients." I ran my fingers through my hair and sat back in my chair. I felt excited for her. "It feels like computer software sales is still your industry of choice, and it will be very lucrative." I opened my eyes, and she was gushing.

"Wow, that's soooo crazy that you say that. I was actually playing around with that idea of starting my own boutique sales agency to provide sales for software companies trying to connect with small businesses. Right now, I'm selling intranet software to businesses so that they can communicate better and manage their workflows. But I'm thinking of moving into the medical field. There's a lot of money in software for hospitals. I can clear 10K or more a month just doing that. I could probably be a consultant for my job too so that I can have more freedom. They have a Miami branch."

"See, the ideas are flowing. Plan it out. Don't procrastinate. Just start working on it now. Nine months is right around the corner."

"Nine months. I love it. It's like giving birth. My business will be my new baby," she laughed. My alarm went off in a soft repetitive beep. Dee frowned.

"Damn. I guess my time is up, huh?"

"I'm afraid it is." My heart raced, but still, I decided to ask. "What are your plans while in town?"

"I'm only here for the weekend. Gonna see my homegirl Storm and her family. But that's not for a little while. Maybe I can convince you to hang out with your favorite client for a little. Maybe get a drink?" She cringed as if waiting for my rejection. "I'll behave this time, I promise. I know you regret what happened that last time I was—"

"Whoa, whoa . . ." I put my hands up. "I never said that I had regrets." I shook my head, blushing from the memory. "It was nice, don't get me wrong, but it's just not professional to cross the line with clients. And the timing wasn't right. But now, I'm . . . I'm single." I actually had a hard time saying it.

"Single?" Dee couldn't even hide her excitement. "Well, well. I'll be damned."

She stood up, and her silver bracelets jingled as she seductively smoothed out the lime sundress that hugged her at the waist and flowed down to her knees.

I shook my head and smiled. Maybe being single isn't as bad as I thought.

She stood over me and tapped my thigh. "Well, let's go. I already know you're hungry."

The front doorbell to my office rang and startled us. "Excuse me." I stood up, but Dee didn't move out of my way. I had to squeeze past her. She was already starting to tempt me.

"Still a big tease," I laughed.

"Oh, I'm not teasing. You *know* I will deliver." She winked.

The hairs on my arms rose.

"I'll be right back. Please, have a seat." My eyebrows rose in delight, and I shook my head as I left her in the room and went out to the lobby to get the door. I saw through the peephole that it was Kylie.

I opened the door and was hit with a surge of her energy full of glowing yellow and white colors. Her aura was always so strong. If I were ever having a bad day, she was the pick-me-up that always made me feel better. It was nice having her work down the hall at the Like a Fly on the Wall Detective Agency.

Kylie's natural hair was full of big curls today, fun and exciting like her personality. She was wearing a jeans skirt, a tight, striped, green and white halter tank, and heels.

"Jacques," she sighed dramatically. "Thank Gaaaawd. You're still here."

"Hey, Kylie. Come in, come in. I was just wrapping up. You look nice. You got a hot date?"

"Nope. I'm meeting my new roommate." We sat down in the waiting room.

"Wow, you're finally moving out of True's spot?"

"Yeah. My mom and I need our space. I've been able to save up a bit now too." She softened her voice. "Are you still in a reading?"

"I just finished."

"Can I get a quick piggyback reading?" She made air quotes as she asked, "You still in the zone?"

I shook my head. Kylie always wanted a "piggyback reading," as she called it. "Just one question" was her line, but it usually was about three questions. I always gave in, because I really loved to help her.

"What's the name?"

"Mackenzie Alexander. She seems cool, but I want to see what you pick up."

I took a deep breath and saw a tall silhouette of a woman in my mind. I felt her energy right away. "Fun, mysterious, a little wild, yet mature. I like her. She sounds like you." I smiled with my eyes closed. I was quiet for a moment as I saw a vision of a woman with an intense focus at a desk like she was studying. That told me she was a deep thinker or in a school of some kind. "Is she in school? Law school? Something intense."

"Damn, you still freak me out. She's a med student."

"Aaaah . . . That explains it. Yes, she is a bit more complicated than you. She has her introverted moments. I think she might be a good match for you, though. I see the two of you getting close. A regular Thelma and Louise. A strong bond. She is very private, but I see her developing trust in you."

Kylie was smiling from ear to ear. "I love how you do this shit soooo fast. I can't wait to meet her now. We talked on the phone already, and I really liked her vibe."

"It's a big space. Feels like you have loads of room and sun. Is it a house?"

"Yes. In Coral Gables. Not too far from here." She glanced at her phone to check the time. "I better go. We're meeting at Annabelle's."

I put my hand on her wrist. "Wait, you wanna know who's here?"

"Who?"

I talked softer. "Dee."

"Noooo way. Whaaaat? Soooo?" She pushed for details.

I whispered, "She came for a reading." I grinned since I knew what she was thinking.

Kylie whispered, "Jacques, you know she likes you. It's been forevaaaa since you broke up with Vicky. Go and have fun already." She playfully slapped my shoulder.

"Well, if you recall, Dee was the reason we broke up."

She sucked her teeth. "That wasn't Dee's fault. You should have deleted the damn text. Have some fun. You deserve it. Get you some cootch already. Have you even been laid since Vicky moved out?"

I shrugged, forcing a smile. I put my finger in front of my mouth to tell her to hush.

Truth was, I was obsessed with work and just not ready for anyone else to be in my space. I'd been out for drinks here and there with a couple of female companions, but I never took it further.

She snickered. "I gotta run to meet Mackenzie."

"Okay. Just come say hello real quick."

We walked over to the room, and I cracked the door. Dee was texting someone and looked up in surprise. "Oh shit, what's up, girl?" She rose from her seat.

"Deeee, you look great. So good to see you." They embraced like long lost friends, although they only met that one time the lights went out in my office.

"I have to run, but please get my info from Jacques and add me on social media."

"Okay, will do. Good to see you." Dee sat back down, and I walked Kylie back to the waiting room.

"Thanks for the piggyback." She kissed me on the cheek and whispered, "You better get you some. Ciao."

I held the door for Dee and let her walk out of the building ahead of me. The sunset was on the horizon, but even after 7:00 p.m., the sun was still blazing hot. The heat hit us at full force as the doors opened.

She caught me checking her out and pretended she didn't. "Which way?"

I pointed to our right. Her grin could not be contained. I admired her confident, smooth stride.

"It's just a few blocks. We're going to go to CocoWalk, then make a right on Grand Street. They have a lot of choices there. Might want to try out this Italian spot, Bice Bistro. Heard it's good."

"Yes, I'd love that. I'm pretty hungry myself." She rubbed her belly.

The décor in the restaurant had a cozy, rustic feel . . . earth tones, exposed brick walls, and dark wood. It was buzzing with the after-work crowd, but thankfully, we didn't have to wait long to be seated. I felt a bit awkward since this was really like a date, as much as I didn't want to think it was. I ran my hand through my hair as the hostess led us to our table.

Dee played with her necklace while looking at the menu. "Oh yes, I'm gonna get the chicken Parmesan. Whatchu getting?"

I pointed to the menu. "This pan-seared salmon with mashed potatoes is looking good."

"Why you keep shaking your leg?"

I looked down. I didn't even realize I was doing it. "Oh, sorry."

"You nervous?"

"Me? Nervous?" I laughed. "Dee, don't be ridiculous. You're beautiful, but I'm okay." I cleared my throat. "I think I'll be okay."

Dee poked her chin up toward me. Her lips parted, and she made firm eye contact. "I knooooow. I'm just teasing you. But I have a confession. Do you know when I first met you, I used to get soooo nervous. Palms would sweat. My heart would jump. All that."

"Why? Scared of what I would tell you in a reading?"

"Well, that too. But you know you have this presence about you. That look." She pointed at my eyes with two fingers. "It's intense, Jacques. It takes time to get used to." She lightly stroked her throat. I found that very sexy.

"Oh, stop it." My face felt warm.

"But now that we're cool, you really aren't as intimidating as you seemed. You are so chill . . . sexy and chill."

"Why, thank you. You're still a bit intimidating, but I think I can handle it."

She slapped my hand, laughing.

I wanted to touch her. I wanted her to sit next to me, like Vicky and I would whenever we sat in booths. I hadn't been that close to anyone in months, and I missed the intimacy. Dee was not Vicky, but she was good company.

My brother Hicham's abrasive tone popped into my head. "Yo, Jaaaay, stop being a bitch. You're single, man. You better fuck the shit out of her tonight . . . 'cause if it were me, I'd handle that shit right now. Fuck all this small talk." I shook my head, trying to clear him out and get focused.

"Jacques, you're staring at me. Are you reading me?"

I licked my lips. "Just relishing in your beauty. I'm not always reading people. I'm off the clock."

"Oh, please, like you can turn it off. Well, you can stop trying to read my mind. You already know how I really feel, but I said I'm not going there. We're going to have a nice, little friendly dinner." Dee dramatically pulled up the menu over her face as if it were shielding her from my psychic powers. Then she lowered it, giggling.

I scanned the menu and softened my voice. "Exactly. A friendly dinner." I looked into her eyes. "This is nice. I don't think we've ever really hung out . . . well, other than the last time."

"No, well, you were on lockdown, so . . ." She squinted. "Soooo, I have to be a little nosy. What happened between you and your girl?"

I could tell she was delighted underneath her concerned pout. I cleared my throat. "Well, it's not my favorite subject, but I'll tell you. Well, if you *really* want to know."

Her voice softened even further. "Yes, I want to know."

I sighed. "She read one of your text messages. At my birthday party in October. I left my phone on the table, and it was just a big mess."

"Oh my God. Which text? What did I say?"

"Well, the one saying you didn't know how fucking passionate I was, or something of that nature. It was pretty bad." I felt my stomach turn, this time not from hunger, but guilt. I hated reliving that night. I had the same sinking feeling in my chest as when Vicky handed me my cell phone that night after reading the text.

She leaned in and whispered, "You didn't even . . . You didn't finish."

I shrugged my shoulders. "Well, we did enough." I raised an eyebrow. "Enough for you to call it passionate." I tried to smile even though I felt bad about it.

Vicky was one of the most sensual and sexually un-inhibited women I had ever been with, but Dee was especially wild and insatiable. She exuded femininity without even trying, and her sassy personality was a welcomed challenge. Something in me wanted to tame her. She was always flirting, but I usually had my barrier up. Now, I would be able to take it as far as I wanted to.

Being my client for several years, I knew her soul. Her stepdad abused her as a teen, which had set her on a path of promiscuity and a string of bad relationships. I knew her fears, lies, dirty secrets, fetishes, sexual encounters, and, yes, like many of my clients . . . she didn't hold back any details. She would feel totally vulnerable if she really knew everything that was revealed to me by my visions.

Over time, I built up quite a lust for her. I always felt guilty for thinking about her in that way, because I knew the root of many of her problems. But the night of the blackout, I gave in to my desires. The whole city being in darkness made it easy. When we snuck away to my office bathroom, I just thought we'd hug, maybe even a simple kiss. Before I knew it, she was down on her knees, pleasuring me. I mean, hands down, she could teach a workshop on giving head. I still get chills when I think about it. It was probably only a few minutes. Then the lights came back on, shining on us in shame. But that unforgettable rendezvous remained imprinted in my mind for months.

A few minutes of lust and a text ruined a two-year relationship just like that. Victoria Morena was a beautiful Puerto Rican from the Bronx. I haven't slept well since she left me. My apartment feels hollow without Vicky's warmth, her cooking, and her music. We were inseparable. I never cheated on her. I've had temptations here and there, but I never crossed the line . . . until Dee.

My good friend, Melissa, who is a psychic, as well, gave me a reading the day after the big breakup. She told me to email Vicky, just tell her everything, and she would forgive me. I tried to write something to her, but it stayed in my drafts for a month before I deleted it. The words never seemed convincing enough. I couldn't manifest the right sentences that would explain Dee's "passionate" text.

I know I deserved it, but I had to stop feeling sorry for myself. I figured hanging with Dee would be fun, and since I got in trouble for it already, I might as well make it worth my while. She would take care of my depression . . . at least for now, I thought.

Our food arrived, and it was pretty tasty.

"Jacques, I'm soooo sorry. It was pretty silly of me to send that text. I just never knew we'd have that much chemistry. I mean . . . I was in shock. You were talking in French and shit. You had me fucked up for months. I ain't even gonna lie." She sat back as if she were savoring the memory. She dangled her pasta on a fork and pointed it at me. "I mean, fucked-up. I was mad too. I felt cheated that we never got to spend more time together, but I get it. You had a situation, and I didn't want to be a home wrecker." She mumbled, "But looks like I did anyway. I'm sorry. Really, I am."

I saw a soft pink glow around her shoulders and chest. Her aura was illuminated. Her heart shined. She was feeling guilty about what happened. It made me want her more.

I took a sip of wine. "Hey, it happened, and a few other things were going on that night that sparked her jealousy, so it wasn't all you. Vicky was a bit drunk, so her temper got the best of her, and, well, one thing led to another. I still feel like an asshole for hurting her," I sighed.

"You really are a good dude. They don't make them like you anymore, Jacques. Real talk."

"Let's change the subject to something lighter, now, shall we?" I raised my eyebrows and tried to switch up the mood by channeling Hicham's playful energy. Trying to be like him was not easy since he didn't have much of a conscience.

"Okay, you're single. I'm single, and I think we'll be great friends." Dee smiled her charming smile.

She put her hand out as if I would shake it. I held it in mine. Then I kissed the top of it. "Friends it is, mon amour."

"Ooooh." She snatched her hand back and rested it on her chest. "Oh noooo, just don't talk in French, and we'll be good."

We laughed.

The awkwardness subsided, and time flew by as we talked more about the results from her reading and her possible life in Miami. Dee stepped away to the bathroom, but on her way back, she made a pit stop at the bar.

"What's that?" I pointed to the shot glasses in her hand that had sugar around the rims.

"Lemon Drop shots. I'm on vacation, and I can't do it alone."

"Oh boy, this doesn't seem like a good idea."

"It's a celebration, bitches," she said in her bad impersonation of Dave Chappelle, impersonating Rick James.

I ran my fingers through my hair. "What are we celebrating, exactly?"

"Well, my new business, us hanging out, and it's been five months since I stopped smoking."

"Wow, seriously? That's awesome, Dee." That reminded me of another thing I didn't like about her before . . . the smoking. "But, ah . . . Are we trading one habit for another?"

"Oh, please, I'm a social drinker. I don't do it that often."

We bumped glasses. "Cheers," we said together.

Dee pointed to my glass. "Wait, you gotta lick the sugar first."

She licked it and waited for me to do the same. Then Dee swallowed the shot like a champ with her head swinging back.

"Well, you're no lightweight, apparently." I copied her and took a big gulp. I was not really into shots, but I figured it would loosen me up. "I prefer red wine."

"Wine is for sissies, and let's face it. I know you are *not* a sissy." Her eyes went below my belt.

I rubbed my hands together, biting my bottom lip. "Starting already?"

"Oh, Jacques, we're just getting started." She laughed and raised her empty shot glass. "Harmless flirting amongst friends."

"Yes, harmless."

"I'm just happy to be alone with you in a fun environment. I always wondered if you ever relaxed. I see you getting all these interviews in *Cosmo* and the *New York Times* and all. Your schedule must be insane."

"Well, it's been a blessing. Some of my clients bragged about me to the right people." I had a celebrity client land a huge movie role based on my suggestions in a reading, and ever since then, the referrals have been a lot of entertainment folks. I actually was trying to lie low about all of the press I've been getting. It's been a little nerve-racking with so many people calling. It's a good problem to have, and I'm very grateful, but it's a lot. "But as far as relaxing, of course, I do. I meditate daily."

"Oh, come oooon. Not meditation. You know, like let your hair down, party, loosen the fuck up."

"Wow, so you think I'm uptight?" I waved my hands over the empty shot glasses on the table. "Is *that* what's happening here?"

She shrugged her shoulders and wrinkled her freckled nose. "What are you again—33, 34?"

"I'm 32."

"Even worse. You act like a responsible 62-year-old. Enjoy yourself a bit."

"Now you sound like my brother."

"Oh, Hickam? The one with the rude-boy relationship blog?"

"Yes, it's pronounced Hee-sham."

She covered her mouth. "Oops, my bad."

"It's fine. He calls it a relationship blog, but there is a lot of tongue-in-cheek humor in it. He has a big fan base, though. Some people actually follow his advice to the letter." I shook my head.

"It's ratchet. I read one or two entries."

"In his mind, he thinks he's a psychologist and a relationship coach."

"Well, I'm not saying to be a man-whore like him, but you could have some fun."

"What's your idea of fun?"

"I'll show you, Jacques. I got you."

Chapter 2

Kylie

I sat anxiously in Annabelle's café, facing the door so that I could see Mackenzie when she walked in. Some groovy jazz played under the light chatter of the college kids. FUI logos adorned their laptops, baseball caps, and T-shirts. So much school pride. I'd been the same way about my alma mater, Columbia. You couldn't tell me nothing.

I looked in my phone to kill time and checked my Facebook notifications. The first meme I saw said,

"Throw me to the wolves and
I'll come back leading the pack."

I smiled. That was me in a nutshell. Hell, I knew a lot about overcoming, and I was proud of my newfound success. Over the last year, my life had been an unpredictable roller coaster of events. After getting laid off from my music-industry job, I had to pack up my swanky Park Slope apartment and move down to Coconut Grove, Florida, to live with my mom. I'd helped her out many times before, but I still had my tail between my legs when I arrived. Thank goodness she had landed a good man (for a change) who owned a beautiful home in a very nice area. Basim was really a savior for both of us. He gave me a sanctuary to collect my thoughts and get back to being myself.

Coming from the NYC rat race to South Florida's chill mode was like day and night. The culture shock forces you to slow down. I slowed down so much I forgot my lump sum severance was going to run out soon. I enjoyed the days at the beach more than looking for a job. It caused a lot of friction between my mom and me, and I knew I had to get out of there soon.

As luck would have it, I landed an office job at Like a Fly on the Wall Detective Agency. It was below my pay grade, but I was desperate and had been promised a raise when I passed the Private Investigator State Exam. It was a lot of busywork, but I was lucky to have a good teacher: Vince. My boss was a retired homicide detective. And there was also Antonio, my tall, dark, and delicious-looking coworker. I busted my ass to prove my worth, and it worked. I was finally living out *Law and Order* episodes and playing detective.

My days were filled with research. I knew being nosy was going to be fun, but busting cheaters and crooks was pure bliss. I'd found my calling. I was *made* for this. Bills were being paid. And Breeze, my New York lover, was being super attentive. I mean, facetiming me daily, being extra sensitive to my feelings, and planning frequent visits to see me. Life was getting better.

The melodic chimes on the café door got my attention, and a long-legged woman walked in. She was about five foot nine. She wore tight, dark jeans with some rips on the thighs and a black and gold T-shirt that said, "*Melanin Magic.*" Her hair was light brown. Long, fluffy waves reached down past her shoulders. Could be hers, a weave, or a wig. I wasn't sure. She stopped in her tracks and tilted her black-rimmed cat eyeglasses down to get a better look at me. I told her I would have on a green and white top.

"Kylie?"

I nodded and stood up. "Hey, Mackenzie." I waved and put out my hand for her to shake it when she pushed it away.

Her sweet, Southern accent was welcoming. "Oh, girl, please, I huuuug."

"Oh, you too? I do it too, but some people think it's weird."

"And those are the people you don't need in your life. Too much negativity." We laughed.

I loved her immediately from our phone call the day before, but this was confirmation. Jacques was so right.

Mackenzie sat down and flipped her hair over her shoulder.

"You are so beautiful," I said to her. She kinda reminded me of Ciara and Beyoncé morphed together with vintage cat glasses.

"Oh, chile, please. You are the adorable one. I love your 'fro too." She raised her hand. "Can I?"

I nodded and leaned in so she could touch it. "Oh, it's soooo soft. I'm natural under this." She flipped her artificial hair. I was right.

"Well, you honestly could have fooled me. Looks real. You wear it well. It fits you."

"Kylie, honey, it iiiis real. I get my wigs made with 100 percent human hair. Brazilian Remy. Top of the line, honey. With my schedule, I don't have time to do my hair. This one's name is Yoncey."

"Oh, like Beyoncé?" I laughed.

"Yes, girl. Being Beyoncé on the right day opens doors. Med school be kicking my ass, chile. I have about ten others."

I was so impressed about school. The wigs, not so much.

"What kind of doctor again?"

"General practice, for now. I might switch to OBGYN, but I'm not sure yet. I'm either at school, studying, or doing an internship. Only one more year of this shit."

"I couldn't do it. Four years was enough for me."

"I hear you. But I gotta heal the world. Leave it to these jokers in Big Pharma . . . They trying to take us all out. I'm on a mission." She took an exaggerated deep breath. "Well, let's get down to biz." Mackenzie pulled out a folder from her big leather Michael Kors bag. She had printed out the application that I filled out online. "First off . . . I love your application. Your job sounds so exciting. Private detective agency?"

"Yes, it's pretty cool. I'm only the office manager and in training to be a PI."

"So, you work long hours? How long are you usually out?"

"It varies. If I have to help with surveillance jobs, then it's longer. But I'm not doing that as much just yet. For the most part, I'm home by seven or eight."

"Oh, that's cool. My only request is when I am studying to keep it kind of quiet. These tests alone cost anywhere from $500 to $1,200, so I'm not trying to fail shit."

"Noooo worries. I'll be quiet as a mouse."

"You have a man? I'm sorry to pry but—"

I laughed. "No, it's okay. I understand. I-I kinda . . . well, not reeeeally," I stammered.

"Hey, it's all good. I just prefer that you let me know if a dude comes over, so I'm not walking in the kitchen in my thong and T-shirt." She peered over her cat glasses. "And as long as he isn't at the house alone, we're good. You will have your own entrance too, so that's covered."

"Wow, that's nice. I did see that in the ad. To answer your question, no. I'm not in a committed relationship, but I do see someone from time to time, but he's up north. I also date, but nothing to write home about." I shrugged.

"Oh, guuuurl . . . How do you doooo that? I can't do long-distance dick. I get to itching and craving. I want it right away." She pretended to scratch her neck and sides of her torso like she was breaking out in crackhead hives. "The lady needs her fix. Okaaaay?"

I cracked up at her Southern drawl. I couldn't stop laughing. "Oh my Gaaawd, you are a damn comedian. I'm just loving your energy."

"Well, the lady needs her maintenance, just like a car. Gotta rotate my tires, get the oil changed. All dat." She framed her body with her hands.

I didn't know if the "lady" she spoke of was herself or her vagina. She seemed to use them interchangeably.

"I agree." I raised my hand as if I were in church testifying.

"Sheeeeit, I always keeps a Negro on the side, just in case. I got needs. But I gotta work on restocking my sides. I just had the worst dick eveeeer. I mean theeee worst." She leaned in and grabbed my arm. "I'm sorry. I know we just met and all, but it's best you get broken in now."

We both started laughing. I begged, "Break me in. Tell me." She was oversharing just a tad, and I was loving it.

Just then, the waitress interrupted us. "Can I get you ladies something?"

"Oh, I'll get green tea, please." I smiled at her.

"I'll do the same, with agave, please."

Mackenzie tilted her glasses and looked at the waitress as she walked away. She whispered to me, "She was all up in it like she wanted to join in. All *up* in the tea."

"Go on with your story. I think it's going to be good." I waved my hand for her to continue.

"Yes, baaaaby, it was a doctor I interned with. My friends at school used to call him 'Doctor Make Yo' Panties Wet.' Gurl, last week, he was 'Doctor Make Yo' Panties Cacklin' Dry.' I mean, shoooot, I was devastated,

Kylie. I just knew it was gonna be gooood. He could kiss, he could dance, and the chemistry on the last few dates was incredible." She threw her hands up. "He's soooo fine too. Looks like an older Michael B. Jordan."

I said, "Damn, what a freakin' waste. And he knows his way around the human anatomy toooo? How'd he mess that up?" I shook my head.

"Please, don't rub it in. I mean, he had me on fire for the last month—all this buildup for nothing. I know I shouldn't be doing all that flirting as an intern. I guess that's what made it fun since it's frowned upon."

"Oh, please, it ain't like you're underage," I snickered. "You're an adult intern."

"I know my old ass. I'm a late bloomer. I figured it's now or never. You know I'm 37?"

"Wow, 37. You don't look it at all," I raved. She could easily pass for 28. I wondered why she started so late.

She laughed. "I wasn't really planning on doing it with him until after this semester was over and I left his hospital, but, child, he was soooo aggressive. I just knew he was gonna give it to me good. Before I even walked in the door to his place, he had my dress hiked up to my belly, was grabbing on my ass, sucking my neck . . . Then he started smelling my hair. I was actually natural that day. I just blew it straight. No wig. But he was all in my hair. I mean, he was like, 'Oh, it smells so good . . . like apricot and lavender.'"

I covered my mouth. "Apricots?"

"Yeah, holding my head close to his nose and shit." She raised her hands like she was about to announce the rest of the story to the entire café. But she lowered her voice. "Then he opened his pants. Guuuurl . . ." She stomped her feet dramatically.

My mouth was open, *craving* details. "What? It was big?"

Mackenzie was so animated, banging the table as she recounted the experience. "No, no, no. Wait." She held her hand up as if stopping traffic. "Guuuurl . . . I could barely find that shit. He had a bush on him from 1978 down there. 1978, I tell ya."

"Oh shit." I was laughing, and I couldn't stop. Tears formed in the corners of my eyes.

She talked fast. "I ain't never seen no mess like that in all my years of fucking, and I've been getting it iiiin for a minute."

"What—it was that bad? You needed a weed whacker and shit?"

"Sheeeeit. That joker could grow dreads and get Rick James's cornrows with that long-ass hair around his little dick. It was a terrible sight—a *terrible* sight." Her accent made her stories that much funnier.

"But . . . You still did it?" I tilted my head, confused. "I would have run up out of there."

"Kylie, how do you get out of something like that? I felt horrible. I was dried up like the Sahara Desert after that."

I screamed. "Yoooo." My cheeks were hurting now from laughing so much.

She rambled on, "I didn't sign up for this shit." She slapped down her hand on the table and laughed at herself.

Then she held her hand up. "Wait . . . I ain't get to the worst part yet. So, I decided just to do it, since we got this far, and he already put the condom on. I didn't even think he was hard all the way when he put it in . . . I didn't feel a thing. I mean, not one. Single. Thing. I thought, maybe it will get bigger or harder. But, no . . . He came in like two minutes. It was soooo bad. He was like a bunny rabbit in a bad porno. He didn't even try to pleasure me. No stroke game. It was all about him."

"Selfish," I mumbled. "That's some shit college boys do. Not a grown-ass man. What the hell?"

"Then everything made sense. His flashiness, cars, gifts, cockiness was just overcompensating. Chile, please. Never again will I do that, doctor or no doctor."

"Damn, don't you have to see him at work now? How do you deal with that?"

"I'm not working on his floor this week, and next week, I rotate out of that hospital. I'll just avoid him. Maybe I will just tell him that we ain't compatible or that I got back with my ex." She twirled her hair into a ponytail and turned to the waitress, who was putting our teas down with a smirk. She *really* wanted to join us.

"Thanks," we said in unison as she walked away.

I wiped the tears from my eyes. "Oh, man, you need to do stand-up. That shit was hilarious. Rick James's hair on a dick? I can't get that visual out of my head now. I see the beads and everything," I laughed. "He was using his hair as a diversion."

"Yeah, ain't nobody that busy that you can't take some time to do a little housekeeping down there." She made imaginary scissors in the air. "Don't nobody wanna see that shit. You know he one of them island mutts mixed with Indian, white, Black, and Chinese. Fine, girl. So, at least it was pretty, soft, wavy hair." She laughed so hard, she snorted.

"Oh, brother. Good dick hair?" I rolled my eyes.

"What? It was pretty, at least. Okay . . . Okay, just picture a finger sticking out of a, I don't know, a Tina Turner or Chaka Khan wig. Yeah, that's it. Picture that shit." She started laughing, and I joined her.

"Yoooo. I can't with you, Mackenzie." My stomach was hurting now from laughing so hard. Everyone in Annabelle's was smiling at us having a good time. It looked as if we'd been friends for years.

"I feel better." She blew out air. "You know, I've been holding that story in for over a week. I can't tell my classmates. They'd be mad at me for fucking one of the teachers."

"It's all good. I'm sure I got some stories for you too. Well, I don't want to assume, but if you decide to choose me . . ."

"Guuurl, you know you in like Flynn. Stop playing. You wanna go check out the house now? You can move in tomorrow."

"Yes, I'd love to. Let's do it."

I really loved my new roommate, Mackenzie. She was like a new big sister. She was so free-spirited and seemed to be hardworking—a lot like me. I was looking forward to this new friendship. If there's one thing I love, it's a go-getter, and it's a plus that she's hysterical.

Chapter 3

Jacques

Three glasses of wine, a Lemon Drop, and two Baby Guinness shots later, I decided I wasn't going to have any more to drink. Dee had the tolerance of a bull. It was like she just had a cup of soda. Not even a bit tipsy.

The music got louder in the restaurant, and Dee was now on my side of the booth showing me funny videos on her Instagram account. I wanted her next to me, so when she offered to sit closer to show me, I didn't mind at all. We were doing everything we could to delay parting ways. She scooted closer to me and gave me the phone to hold. She had one hand on the phone, and I put my hand on it as well to hold it up. When our fingers brushed, I got the tingles. Her dress exposed her thighs a bit when she sat down. I put my right hand under the table and slowly rested it on her thigh and squeezed it.

"Oh, see, you crossing that friend zone, Jacques," Dee warned me with puckered lips.

"What? Just watching this video with you," I smiled. My eyes felt heavy.

"You're drunk. Damn, Jacques, I didn't know you were a lightweight like that. You can't drive home now."

I sat up straight. "I'm not drunk. From those little sips?" I leaned into her neck and said softly. "You smell gooood."

Dee giggled, "Yep, you're drunk." She had a look of concern, but I didn't feel drunk—just a little light-headed and extra horny.

I laughed. "What wrong? I just like you. I enjoy you. Something wrong with that?" I said softly in her ear while squeezing her leg again. My hardness was bursting through my pants.

I heard Kylie's voice in my head. *"You need to get you some cootch."* I wanted to ask my spirit guides if they thought it would be a good move, but the alcohol was starting to take over, and my senses were clouded over by lust. I just pictured Dee spreading her legs and me climbing on top of her.

I asked softly, "Where . . . Where are you staying?"

"The Mandarin Oriental in Brickell." Our faces were close. "Why?" She looked at my lips and softly into my eyes. Then she took a deep breath as if she were trying to compose herself. "I'm sending you home in an Uber. I don't want you talking about how I took advantage of you." The funny video stopped, and she put the phone down.

"Oh, that won't happen. I'm fine. I want to just relax with you. I haven't . . . I haven't been out in a while."

"Well, you know, I'm not going to say no to you."

I lightly touched her chin and gave her a quick kiss on the lips. "Good. Let's go." She looked surprised and leaned in for more, not seeming to care about other people in the restaurant. I grabbed both sides of her face and pulled her in for a deep, sensual kiss. I could taste the Baileys on her tongue. She moaned softly, kissing me back and grabbed my thigh. I moved her hand to my crotch and held it there.

She giggled. "Jacques, Jacques, chill out."

I said low, "No one can see under the table. You're the one making it obvious. Everyone is minding their business eating their food. Now, who is the uptight one, huh?" I teased.

Dee was laughing hysterically, and her laugh was infectious. I laughed with her.

"You play too much. I'm calling us a damn Uber. You not gonna embarrass me up in these streets."

"Meeee? Embarrass you?" I let my fingers crawl up her leg and under her dress. I squeezed the inside of her thigh. It was moist from the heat growing in between her legs. I knew I was going to have her tonight. I spoke tenderly in her ear. "Sorry, it's been awhile."

"Oh, please. I know you got chicks throwing it at you *all day*."

"Maybe." I grinned and touched her chin. "That doesn't mean I want to catch everything being thrown." I looked into her eyes and lightly tugged on her bottom lip. The heat between us was intense. We noticed eyes on us. I grinned at the booth in front of us, acknowledging an older couple staring at us. "We should go." I felt slightly light-headed, but I figured if I lay down for a bit, I would be fine, and her body was perfect to lie next to.

Dee quickly pulled up the Uber app on her phone. "Oh, good. He'll be here in two minutes."

I was no longer nervous and very, very aroused. I was looking forward to spending more time with her and finishing what we started.

The hotel room was elegant and cozy with soft track lighting.

"You gotta check this out." She opened the sliding door, and the view was breathtaking. The entire downtown Miami skyline was illuminated. We were up twenty-one floors, and I started to feel a little uneasy. "Let's just stay here. I felt a bit woozy." Slowly, I walked back to the bed.

"Okay, you're tired, huh?" She gave me a sly look. "I'll be right back."

She went into the bathroom, and I sat up on the side of the bed and turned on the TV. "Want to watch a movie?" I yelled while channel surfing with the remote.

When she didn't respond, I figured she didn't hear me. Five minutes went by, and then she came out of the bathroom in a black lace G-string and bra. I jerked my head back.

She slowly walked toward me. "Sure. What movie you wanna watch?"

Her body was magnificent. I mean, I had no idea she was going to look that good naked. She was toned like a dancer: plump breasts, flat stomach, round ass. I felt a rush of adrenaline racing through my body. I was so happy I brought a condom.

I lost all inhibitions. "Come *here*."

"What? I thought you wanted to watch a movie?" She stood in front of the large, flat-screen TV. The blue glow was a spotlight on her, highlighting all of her curves. Her confidence was turning me on. "What channel you want? PG, R, or Rated XXX?"

I was trying my hardest to compose myself and not just get up and rip off her underwear. I nervously scratched my head. "Aaaah, Rated X, please." We were playing a dirty little game, and I loved it.

She slowly walked up to me, bent down, and whispered in my ear while poking out her butt, "I'm going to need that remote so that the show can begin."

I slapped her ass and smiled like a child about to get a huge present. The sharp sting did nothing to her. "Ooooh, you like that? I got more for you."

She skipped away from me, and I enjoyed watching it bounce. She was teasing me so well; I didn't know what to do. Dee dimmed the lights and used the remote to switch the TV to a channel that played R&B music. "Okay, the show is going to start now." A slow Usher song started, and she swayed side to side and began dancing slowly around the bed. She'd come close, but not close enough. She was very good at this game of seduction. Dee was playing with her bra straps as if she were going to take them off.

I sat back and just enjoyed how she was making me crave her. She came closer to me and danced in front of me, winding her body around as if she were dancing to reggae. Dee stooped down a few times to kiss me and then smoothly backed away. She'd done this before, I thought. She played with my hair and blew gently in my ear. Dee shimmied her soft breasts in my face, then pulled away as I caressed them. She turned around and bent down touching the floor, came back up, and shimmied her butt like a stripper. It was then I had to grab her onto my lap to put the teasing to a halt.

"Okay, okaaaay, that's enough." I shook my head as I held her body close to mine. Then I put my hands in between her legs. "I can't take it anymore." My voice dropped an octave deeper. "*Je veux te faire l'amour maintenant.*"

"Shit, Jacques, I *really* like this side of you," she whispered. "You got condoms?"

I said sternly, "Oh, now would *not* be the time to ask, but, yes, I do, and I'm going to fuck the shit out of you."

She sat in my lap, and I ripped her panties off a little rougher than I expected.

"Damn, Jacques."

Her eagerness joined mine, and she got up and started helping me get out of my pants. I removed her bra.

"Oh, you know I'm gonna take care of you first, right?" She stroked my hardness that was poking at full attention. "We never got to finish last time."

"Please, please, take care of me," I sighed as I shook off my pants leg.

"Look at the big dick you got. Ooooh, I'm going to enjoy thiiiis." Dee got on her knees and flickered her tongue on the tip as a preview.

She had a sinister smile as if she knew I were under her spell. She knew I remembered how good she was too. Dee gently grabbed me and began sucking me at full length. She stroked with both hands. She was loud, groaning, sucking, and exuding so much pent-up passion. It was overwhelming. My head was spinning from the alcohol, and I was in complete ecstasy. She was giving it all she had. I took a few deep breaths, trying to keep my composure as I watched her. Dee was using all kinds of tricks and movements that were completely new to me. I felt like I was about to explode, but I didn't want to end without finishing the job. I wanted to savor her and finally see what it would feel like.

I gently tapped her shoulder to stop. I pulled her closer to me and then tossed her naked body beneath me. Her eyes widened from my forcefulness. She loved it. I took off my top, and she started kissing my neck and chest. She was so insatiable and wanted to please me in every way. My heart sped up. I fumbled with the condom. She spread her legs and sighed, "Shit, Jacques, I've been waiting for this. You don't even knoooow."

I entered her slow and deep to silence her. She dug her fingers into my back as if we were going to melt into each other. She felt so good, so warm. I couldn't believe I waited this long to do this.

"Shit, Dee. You know how good you feel? You know?"

"No, noooo. Tell me in French," she begged. The sweat on her skin glistened.

My voice was deep and steady, *"Tu es si sexy . . . Je pourrais te baiser toute la journee.* You are soooo sexy. I didn't know you would be this good. I could fuck you all day. *Je ne savais pas que tu serais si bonne.* All daaaay I want to be inside you. *Ouvrir,*" I panted. "Come on . . . Open your legs more." I stroked her slow as the heat between our bodies was building. We were covered in sweat. I saw a tear come out of the corner of one of her eyes, and she looked away. My confidence rose further, and I took my time with her. "Ah . . . I see you like this. You like this dick, don't you?"

She was breathing softly and gyrating her hips to meet mine at a smooth and steady pace. I said in her ear, "I caaaan't hear you, Delilaaaah." She moaned softly, and it sent waves down my back.

When I looked into her eyes, I saw someone else. A young Indian girl . . . almost like a hologram over Dee's face. Her hair was long, and her skin tone a deep chocolate. She had a *bindi* on her forehead. It was the strangest thing. Goose pimples formed on my arms and the back of my neck. I thought the liquor was making me see things. I touched the side of her face with the back of my hand, and the vision disappeared. Her skin was smooth. Even at 35, she was fresh-faced like a college senior.

I got on my knees and pulled her legs up high over my shoulders and entered her again . . . this time with swift force. I wasn't gentle. I knew she liked it rough. She screamed, "Shit, Jacques. Yessss. Yessss. I love it. I love this shiiiit." Her legs clenched on to my neck tightly. Our bodies rocked together to the R&B grooves playing in the background.

Just then, I felt my body release. "Uuuugh." Dee's legs were vibrating over my shoulders. I had to hold on tight. I turned my head to kiss her ankle.

"Fuck, I haven't come like that in years. Years. You done messed up now, Jacques." She laughed as her body collapsed next to me, and she playfully slapped me on my butt.

I don't know why, but I got nervous from that remark, that playful threat. *"You done messed up now."* I remember my brother writing an article one time about never giving women your all the first time you have sex because they will become obsessed. I hoped that I didn't do that. However, I honestly don't know how you can hold back. I *have* to give it my all. I've never been a selfish lover.

I lay next to her. "Why did I mess up now?" I played dumb.

"You know you gave me that gooood psychic dick," she laughed. "That shit was waaaay better than I thought it was gonna be. Goddamn."

"Psychic dick? Now *that's* funny."

She slowly got up. I smiled, watching her walk to the bathroom ever so carefully. Next, I heard the shower running.

I took a shower after she did, and we cuddled in the aftermath of bliss. Aside from the downtown skyscrapers, the moon and stars outside, there was an indigo glow from the TV. The screen showed a photo of the group Guys' first album as their hit song "I Like" played in the background.

"So, I know we aren't in a reading, but I want your opinion . . . as a man. Why do you think I'm still single? Is there something about me?"

"Well, you know you're a catch, Dee, but you just haven't let go of some things that happened in the past, and, well—"

She abruptly interrupted me. "You mean my stepdad molesting me . . . *raping* me?"

I blinked hard. "Well, yeah, I didn't want to say that, but also your mother not believing you when you finally told her. I know it's had an impact on you trusting people—even after therapy."

"Yep, you're right. It does still hurt." She sighed. "Even after my mom and I made up, I'm still angry about it. You can't just let go of that shit. I mean, I try, but . . ." She played footsies with me. "Do you think I'm going to be single forever?" She stroked my chest hair and tangled her leg into mine.

"Noooo, not at all. What I remember in your readings is you just haven't been around the right men."

"Yeah, you do know me so well . . . reformed thugs or sales guys who act like misogynist jocks. I'm sick of those types now. I used to love cocky men." She stared up at the ceiling and stretched out more. "Soooo, what kind of guy you think would be right for me, Jacques?"

I gulped. Was she sending me a hint?

"One who can handle you." I palmed her ass with one hand. "Someone with some backbone and thick skin to handle that sharp tongue of yours." She stuck her tongue out at me like a child. "But someone who will also give you the freedom to be yourself."

Her eyebrows rose, and she cuddled into me more. She was getting sleepy now.

I continued, "We all know you can't be confined in a box or be tamed."

"But I actually like a guy who *can* tame me. That shit turns me on."

I was feeling groggy and speaking a bit slower. I yawned. "You say that now. I know after a while, if they take it too far, you will resent them. Needs to be a balance."

"Are you looking to tame me?" She put her finger on my bottom lip and gazed into my eyes.

I looked away and paused, trying to find the right words. "No, no, that is a job for whoever your next man is. The right one is coming. You know?" I felt like a jerk. It was an awkward thing to say, but I didn't want to lead her on. She told me herself she wanted to be friends.

I felt her energy shift. Her voice got softer as she tried to come back from my gentle verbal blow. "I agree. And it's no time to mess around and get dick-matized." She touched my limp manhood, and it suddenly started to awaken.

I shook my head and leaned my forehead into hers. I spoke right next to her lips. "What the hell was in that shot? My head is officially spinning." I felt a bit sluggish and so aroused again. "I don't drink like this. I told you. Did you drug me?" I gently tapped her on the nose.

Her voice was sultry and relaxed. "Now, why would I do that to you? I want you to remember everything. Every minute you were with me."

I pulled her on top of me. "Oh, I will. Every minute." I grabbed her bottom and started to open her legs and then realized I didn't have a condom on. I remembered she was not Vicky. I tossed her slowly back next to me.

She said, "I don't trust people." She turned her head from me and said softly, "But I . . . I trust you, Jacques."

I didn't know if that was some sort of sign she wanted to do it unprotected, but I didn't care. That was definitely *not* happening. I was slightly drunk, but not out of my mind.

She exhaled and gazed into my eyes, biting her bottom lip. She was so sexy and knew how to look at me just right. Her face was sincere . . . eyes were innocent.

"I feel so good with you," she said.

"Me too. I really haven't had a night where the time flew by so fast, where I laughed so much, where I felt like a teenager again." I looked for the other condom on the dresser to make sure I had it. Relief took over me. Dee softly grabbed my hand and kissed the inside of my palm. It tingled. She sucked on a few of my fingers as if she were giving me a blow job. I started to get hard again.

With a sly grin, she said, "Want to again?"

I got on top of her and began slowly kissing her neck, breasts, and her stomach. Dee's skin was so delicate and smooth. I enjoyed teasing her with my tongue. Her sighs brought me to full excitement. She opened her legs as if a command for me to continue further. I wanted to please her since she worked so hard at pleasing me. I wanted her to forget about her past. I wanted her to feel loved, even if it were just for tonight.

I spread her legs and went down to feast on her. I had a few tricks up my sleeve as well. She sighed as I licked, sucked, and fingered her simultaneously. Her hands clutched my hair. "Oh, damn, damn yoooou, Jacques. Fuuuuck."

She continued to curse me out in indescribable words, and I continued to pleasure her until we fell asleep in each other's arms. I was glad I followed Kylie's advice. Dee was definitely a cure for my loneliness. I needed that.

Chapter 4

Jacques

I was awakened just before dawn when Dee changed positions in her sleep. She soon settled into a cozy spot and laid her small hand on my chest. Her soft breathing, her warm body snuggled up next to mine gave me a sense of peace. I loved making her feel safe and cherished. I had this strong desire to protect her. Even if we were not going in the direction of a relationship, I did care about her.

I thought about how far I'd come in the last months. If there was a bright side to my breakup with Vicky, it was the fact that I focused on myself more. I'd been going extremely hard in the gym to release pent-up stress. I cut out red meat and chicken altogether and was going to attempt a vegan diet for ninety days. I had seen a tremendous shift in my intuition from just eating cleaner, so I knew being vegetarian or vegan would take me to a new level. Many of my psychic friends claimed a plant-based life had detoxified their pineal glands and increased their abilities. So, I figured, why not?

I already had more energy. My six-pack was almost an eight-pack. Dee seemed very impressed, and I was glad to showcase my abs to someone other than the ladies at the gym or beach. I'd been overwhelmed with a lot of new clients due to the latest articles written up about me, but my new virtual assistant, Zoe, was a godsend. We'd only met via Skype, but she had been so good with booking clients and returning calls for me. I used to have people waiting at least a week for a return call. My career was truly at the highest level it had ever been.

One of my spirit guides named Edna, said, "You teach people how to fly when they didn't even know they had wings." That stayed with me since I know I have to follow my dream of helping others on a large scale. Still, the fear of being well known wraps around my throat and shakes me to my core. I didn't want to be put in that "magical mind-reader" box. I didn't want to be put on display like an entertainment freak show.

There is still a huge part of me that fears being judged. Even now, I could hear my mother's voice shouting at me, *"You need to stop this nonsense. That is not a job. I didn't send you to a university to play with spirits."*

Dee began tossing again. She turned away from me, poking her bottom in my direction. If she weren't so deeply asleep, I would take her again. But I just cuddled on her.

I also fell into a deep sleep. And in my dreams, I saw her again—the little Indian girl that was like a flash of a hologram over Dee's face. However, now, I saw myself as a young East Indian man around 18 or so.

I was watching her serve food to the emperor. Ten other beautiful young women surrounded her, and several others were walking around, playing instruments, and dancing. It was a beautiful sight of vibrant reds, golds, greens, and yellows in silk and satin. The emperor lay on a plush bed, surrounded by pillows adorned with gold flower designs, tassels, and tiny mirrors. The women surrounded him as if he were the only man alive. Their eyes were bright and glossy, painted with dark makeup to enhance their beauty even more. The smiles were bright, yet not genuine. None of them wanted to be there.

I approached with a jug of freshwater and a tray of fruits. My throat was growing thick, and my face was flushed. I couldn't bear to watch her pretend to be in love with him. She stood behind him, massaging his shoulders while talking in his ear. Many concubines wished to be one of his favorites, as she was. She giggled and seemed entertained by his bad jokes. Then she looked at me with a curt nod.

Her name was Saasha, and I was Rohan. At only 15, she was now a woman. Sold as a very young girl by her parents, she was now a concubine to the emperor. Her childhood had been stolen.

I'd seen her evolve into who she was not. My father was a warrior for the emperor's army, who was murdered in battle years ago. Because of his bravery, I was spared castration, yet allowed to be a servant in the palace. I just pretended not to be interested in women, so they never saw me as a threat. I was also a carpenter and very handy, so I was always needed around the palace. They hoped I would become a builder one day and continue to expand the palace's territory.

Over the years, Saasha and I snuck moments alone, and our friendship grew. I wanted to save her. Even though she lived a life of luxury, she was still a slave. The other women in the harem were very cruel and jealous of her. They saw her as competition for one of the spots to be his next wife. The punishment for betraying the emperor was certain death, but it was a risk I was willing to take. I was in love.

We planned to hide in the forest that night, where I had a horse waiting. She had stashed a long, hooded robe in the women's quarters so that she could exit without being noticed. I sat outside the castle at an unmanned gate.

I waited for hours. Nothing. The birds started to chirp, and the sun was beginning to rise. She never came. The sounds of elephants trumpeting startled me. I turned around, and two guards grabbed me from behind. In a scolding tone, one of them questioned, "What are you doing here? Why aren't you in your quarters, Rohan?"

My voice was shaky. "I was guarding the gate. No one was here."

They both laughed. "You? Guarding? You're a mere servant. Your father might have been a fighter, but you are no fighter. You were almost made into a eunuch." They continued laughing.

Then we all were startled from the loud screaming coming from the concubine quarters. Suddenly, a parade of footsteps came racing toward us. It seemed like at least thirty women were walking toward us, almost running, and they weren't alone. The emperor was leading the way as he dragged my precious Saasha with him.

His booming baritone frightened me to my core. "You see this?" He shook Saasha and shouted in her face. "All that I've done for you, and this dirty peasant is whom you decided to lie with? Rohan? I was going to make you an empress, Saasha." The ladies behind him gasped. "I took you from one of the poorest villages. I gave your parents a nice place to live and land in exchange for you, and this is how you repay me? You were supposed to be mine."

He charged closer to me. Warm urine ran down my leg. The guards' grip on me got stronger as if they were restraining me from hitting the emperor, even though I made no move to fight back. My body was shaking.

He spit in my face, then pushed me back. "This is the man—no, the boy—you want? You will see how much he loves you now . . . ah. Let us see." He looked at her and gave a menacing smile. "Rohan, your life or hers? What will it be?" His eyes were like black coals staring into my soul. He exuded pure evil.

I cried, "Please, Emperor, have mercy on us."

"Mercy? Disloyalty deserves no mercy. You should have planned better. How far do you really think you would have gotten? Every corner of my land is guarded. Look above you, fool." We all looked up, and there was a guard in a high tower that I had failed to see. He must have alerted the emperor.

The emperor pulled out his sword in one swift movement, and Saasha screamed as he aimed it at me. "Please, don't hurt him. I'm begging you. He is innocent. He is my friend," she wailed.

"Answer me, boy—your life or hers?"

I looked at Saasha with regretful eyes. I knew I would be lucky to be left alive. Surely, they would never let me stay in the palace. My life was worthless.

I shouted like the man I hoped to be one day. "Kill me. Kill me now." My legs were wobbling, so I fell to my knees. "Let her live and kill me." My voice cracked. "I'm sorry for betraying you. She did nothing wrong."

He laughed at my groveling and raised his sword again, and before it could come down on me, Saasha attempted to wrestle it from his mighty grasp. He was a broad and tall man towering over her petite frame. Shocked at her defiance, he pulled her arm and slammed her to the ground like a rag doll. "Lie there and don't move. You don't move."

My heart sank as I feared we both would lose our lives. "Let her go, please," I cried and lurched forward. The guards grabbed me back.

She was sobbing softly. Her face was most certainly bruised after that hard fall she took. The emperor rested one foot on her back to hold her in place. Then he used his other foot to kick out her arm. Everyone screamed in horror as his sword came crashing down with brute force, cutting into her wrist. He raised the sword again and came down for a second time and made a clean chop.

My heart tightened. Blood sprayed the ground and our feet, and she wailed a long, sorrowful cry.

Many of the women in the crowd scattered and cried. A few rushed to help her, using their saris to stop the blood.

The emperor proudly held up his weapon dripping in Saasha's blood and yelled to the crowd. "Let that be a lesson to all who betray me. Let that be a lesson. Should it ever cross your mind that you wish to escape, remember this night." He turned around, dripping in sweat and blood, looking for someone to say something. There was no remorse from this madman.

My hands shook, and I began to cry. I wanted to take the pain away from Saasha, but I couldn't. Her screams shook through me and echoed through the night sky. I could only pray for us all.

He narrowed his eyes in my direction. His voice was cold and deep. "And you, Rohan? You will get your wish."

Still in agony curled up on the floor, Saasha looked at me, knowing the end was near. One of the older women tried to cover Saasha's view so that she wouldn't see what was about to occur.

My stomach churned as he lifted his sword again. The guards suddenly dropped me to the ground, and in less than a second, the emperor's sword plummeted straight into my throat. A sharp, burning pain filled my body as *my lungs quickly flooded with blood, causing me to feel as if I were drowning. And then the hard kicks to my head kept coming. The guards kicked my face, my neck, and ears and shouted as if they were playing a game. The strong metallic taste of blood filled my mouth—and then . . . nothing—blackness.*

I woke up covered in sweat. Dee was shaking me as she kneeled above me on the bed.

"Jacques, are you okay? Are you okay? You need water? You were choking up a storm."

I blinked slowly, getting adjusted to being back in modern times. The room was bright white. We sat up with the sheets still wrapped around us. I grabbed her right wrist. The same wrist always adorned with silver bracelets. My hands trembled. There was a strange discoloration on her wrist.

My voice cracked. "What is that?" I said in a panic. "When did you get that?" The terror of the emperor dismembering Saasha was so fresh. I was still in shock.

"What, this?" She pointed to her wrist. "Jacques, it's a birthmark." She laughed. "Why you tripping? What's wrong with you? You were having a serious-ass nightmare. Scared the shit out of me. You were mumbling 'kill me, kill me.'" She shook her head. "Damn, if that's what y'all psychics dream about, you can keep all them powers." She laughed a throaty laugh and got up off the bed.

I grabbed my head with both hands and took several deep breaths, trying to ground myself. I finally understood the message.

She rubbed my head and neck, trying to relax me. "Do you remember what you were dreaming about?"

"Yes . . . Yes. It was about us."

Dee was taken aback. "So, wait—that nightmare you had was about *us*?"

"Well, it was a bit jarring. It all makes so much sense now. Well, how we get along—why we click."

I went on to tell her what I remembered from the dream, and her eyes bulged as she hung off of every word as I gave her a glimpse into the life of Saasha and Rohan.

"Wow, so you tried to help me escape, and we both died? That's so messed up."

My eyes widened. "Yes, and your birthmark." I gently took her wrist. "It's a sign. It's where that emperor cut you. I don't think you died, though."

"Can you find out more? I want to know more."

I took a deep breath and tapped her leg. "Maybe later." I was afraid I might have said too much. Yes, I do believe my dream meant something. We were soul mates, but not exclusive to each other. We all have soul mates and travel in soul groups. I'm convinced of this from my work. But I feel in this lifetime, my job is to help Saasha/Dee heal, not be her mate.

My phone buzzed on the nightstand. It was Vicky.

Suddenly I had a mixture of joy and guilt. I read the text message.

Hey, Jacques, sorry I missed your call a few days ago. Let's talk. I have something important I want to discuss with you.

She always used to call me Papi. I missed that . . .

Jacques: Sure, I'd like that.

My stomach swirled with nerves.

Vicky: Sunday, 5:00 p.m.?

Jacques: Yes, at the house?

Vicky: Let's meet at Big Pink's. Supposed to be nice this weekend.

Jacques: Okay, see you then. Looking forward to seeing you.

She didn't reply. Dinner was a step in the right direction. I had no clue what she wanted to talk about. But the mere thought of being in her presence had me walking on eggshells. I missed her so much, and I knew I was still in love with her, but I didn't know how many more ways to say sorry for my fuckup.

My stomach was in knots. I hoped that she actually wanted to get back together. If she moved back in, I'd just propose. I didn't want to lose her again. But her not coming to the house was still playing the tough guy. Meeting on neutral ground, in public? I get it. I think she knew our chemistry was too strong to be alone, and she didn't want to give in.

Dee watched me texting and daydreaming. I honestly forgot I had this beautiful naked woman in the bedroom with me.

She was under the sheets and mumbled, "Someone sure seems busy. You OK?"

"Sorry. Just clients sending me updates. I drifted for a minute. Forgive me." I chuckled, trying to erase the vision of Vicky.

"Updates, huh? You must hear crazy shit all day."

"Oh, it's never a dull moment, that's for sure. People wonder why I don't go to the movies as much. My job is free entertainment."

I looked into her eyes and patted her thigh. "Look, it's getting late, and I gotta get my day started."

"No, I hear you. I gotta go hang with my girl, Storm. That's why I'm here. You were just the bonus." We laughed together.

"You mind? I'm gonna freshen up." I pointed to the bathroom.

"Go ahead. It's only 10:00 a.m. I'm gonna meet up with her in a few."

I showered and kept thinking about Saasha, how vivid that memory was . . . How I saw her face flash on Dee's last night. That was new to me. I had never before had anything like that happen.

No wonder Dee had issues with men—being sold into slavery by her own parents, being a concubine, and I'm sure she had other lives that followed similar paths of abuse. I wondered too if losing love in that life trauma-tized my soul as well. Was this maybe the reason I had a hard time moving forward to the next stage with Vicky?

Chapter 5

Kylie

I loved my new spot. Just a few things left to pick up at Mom's, and then I would be 100 percent moved in and settled. Sunlight shined through the tall glass doors. The view of the garden and the melodic song of the birds made me feel as if our house were in a South American forest . . . or on some exotic island. I walked into the kitchen, smiling at a text from Breeze.

Breeze: What's up, sexy? You good? I miss your smile. You gonna let me see a little something tonight?
Kylie: Hey, you. Maybe. LOL. I'll facetime later.

I also responded to a text from my "internet man," Chauncey. We met five months ago online and have seen each other a few times a month. It's the first time I really liked someone in Florida. However, he played hard to get a bit too much for me. It was beyond frustrating.

Chauncey: You been kinda distant lately. How you feeling?
Kylie: Backed up. Lol

Chauncey: Oh, come on, we're still getting to know each other. Girls don't say backed up either.

Kylie: Well, this one does. I'd say I know you enough by now, Chauncey. This is a bit ridiculous. Lol.

Chauncey: I'm at work. I'm gonna call you later, okay? Just be patient. I care about you. I wanna do this right.

Kylie: Okaaaay. TTYL

My bestie, Olivia, said I needed to stop entertaining Chauncey. "Girl, it's been over ninety days and still no dick? This is *not* about being respectable. He's either gay or has numerous STDs." Olivia swore everyone single had AIDS, herpes, or HPV. "Syphilis is even making a comeback. I saw a video on YouTube about it."

Olivia would drive me crazy sometimes, but I just let her ramble on. Part of me was really enjoying the friendship Chauncey and I were building. He was courting me. He treated me like a lady, so I knew I shouldn't be complaining. I was gonna wait just a bit longer, especially since our first date was so hot and heavy. And in the meantime, I had Breeze, who'd been visiting me at least once a month. Imported penis will keep you patient.

I opened the fridge and looked at my two dedicated shelves. They were somewhat orderly, but nothing compared to Mackenzie's squeaky-clean jars and bottles. She may be going to med school, but our fridge was packed with third world potions. It looked like I lived with African shamans. I liked to call them "Mackenzie's Concoctions." All labels faced forward. Wiped clean. Not one drop of syrup, sauce, or liquid of any kind evident. The shelves were immaculate. I was nervous about putting anything in the fridge not closed properly or dripping on the side. To put it simply, the fridge was sterile. It was also full of healthy veggies and vibrant colors. What she didn't grow outside in the back, she picked up religiously every Saturday at the local Farmer's Market.

If a hurricane ever hit us, we were good for a good month with all the food in the fridge and freezer. I peeked out the back and was surprised to find Mackenzie at home in the garden.

"Hey, girl, what's up?"

"Morning, lady. Where you headed?"

"On my way to work. But I got some bad news last night 'cause I heard one of my high school classmates passed away. Only 27 years old. Damn. He was so sweet. Had a daughter."

"Oh no. I'm so sorry, Kylie. What happened to him?"

"Heart attack. He was pretty overweight all his life. So sad."

Mackenzie said, "Black people keep killing themselves. I mean, soul food ain't right for the soul. It ain't healthy."

"He was Puerto Rican."

"Same shit," she chuckled. "Them slave ships just dropped us off at different ports. Everything in Texas is greasy and big. The serving sizes are made for big 300-pound men. But we think it's good. Oh yeaaaah, we're getting a good deal. We run to the buffets and soul food takeouts, eating stuff that were scraps given to slaves once upon a time. Pig feet, chitlins, all that mess. Meanwhile, massa up in there on his throne, eating chicken, fish, and greens."

Mackenzie was one of those conspiracy theorists who had an answer for everything, but she was right.

"Chile, I can't wait till they give me a license to practice medicine as a doctor. I will work my hardest at educating my patients. I might even do workshops in my office. We gotta shift the mind-set of the people. Prescription drugs are not the answer. This . . ." She stretched her arms, covered in long, pink gardener's gloves, over the plants in the backyard. "*This* is the answer. We gotta learn to teach others how to live off the land. You know? How our forefathers did. They sure as hell didn't have Whole Foods or Trader Joe's."

A health activist, an immaculate housekeeper, a devoted gardener, and a woman who can make spaghetti sauce from scratch? When I said I struck gold with this roommate, I hit the jackpot.

"I hear you, and you're right."

"What you gonna do if they call martial law? If a race war breaks out? If they shut down the stores?"

"Oh, Mackenzie, you thinking too crazy—that will never happen."

"You never know. I just like having our own shit."

She showed me barrels on the side of the house that collected rainwater. They had a spout at the bottom so we could drain them. I was beyond impressed.

"You got a piece?"

"You mean, a gun? Noooo."

"Well, I'ma introduce you to my friend, Justin."

"Justin?"

"Yep, Justin, for 'Just in case.' I always got one in the chamber waiting on a mofo to try me," she laughed. "We are women in this house, so we need it."

"Wow, you are not playing, Mackenzie. You know your ass is crazy, right?"

I will *definitely* stay on her good side. She was a true rebel, this one.

"Texas is an open-carry state, so I beeeen had my license."

"Damn, were you ever in a catastrophe or some shit? Was your dad in the military?"

"Nah, but, honey, I've lived. I've had to make it on my own and survive in some hard times . . ." Her voice trailed into almost a mumble.

I felt a slight chill and a prickling of my scalp when she said that. I wondered what made her so scared.

"How long have you lived alone?"

"Most of my life. Been on my own since 17, but I was married for a bit too. It didn't last long. So, now, I'm here." She moved her bangs out of her face with her forearms and pointed. "This here is butter lettuce."

As much as she loved to talk, it was usually about the present and future. I noticed whenever her past came up, she changed the subject fast. Very strange.

Mackenzie smiled. "Oooh, chile, I got some sweet potatoes here." She pointed to another bush. "That there is ginger growing in the ground. If you ever need fresh herbs, just let me know. I got sage, cilantro, rosemary, and basil. They are so finicky. I gotta watch them babies. You can't let them dry up." She picked up a scrawny tomato with claw marks. "My tomatoes are struggling." A squirrel ran up the tree, and she pointed at him. "Them jokers keep sinking their rotten teeth into my shit. It's either them, raccoons, or rats."

"What . . . rats?" I looked down near my feet.

"Girl, you see how much food is out here? They come out. I ain't never seen them with my own eyes, but I hear them. I know they out here. Definitely field mice, at least."

I shivered at the thought.

"Why are you going to work on a Sunday morning anyway?"

"Believe it or not, work. I got a lot of research I need to finish before Monday."

"Catch them cheaters, girl."

We laughed and waved as I walked back in to the front door. "See you, girl."

***

What a long day at work. I was doing mainly research and the paperwork the guys hated doing. I looked out the window at the palm trees dancing in the cool evening wind. Coconut Grove was buzzing with tourists and evening shoppers, even on a Sunday night. I pulled my gaze back to the computer screen and smiled in delightful revenge. I was trying to figure out a diplomatic way to say, "We caught your nasty whore-of-a-wife with not *one* but *three* different men in one week. Photos attached. File for a divorce . . . *pronto.*" Of course, we couldn't advise our clients on what they should do with the information we find. We just collected the facts and presented them, the names, times, locations, photos, and screen shots when possible. However, it brought me much joy to tell our sweet 74-year-old client, Mr. Carter Sullivan, that his young wife was definitely just using him for his newspaper publishing empire and American citizenship. Believe it or not, women are stepping it up more than we know in the infidelity department.

The scandals that we get at Like a Fly on the Wall Detective Agency are heartbreaking, and it makes me wonder if there are any folks out here *not* cheating. We get cases for basic background checking, insurance fraud, company embezzlements, and much more, but cheeeeaaaating? Oh man, cheating seems always to be the breadwinner when we do the company's financial income statement each month.

My boss, lead Private Investigator Vince Salvatore, truly supports my career growth. I just love that I am actually an assistant detective in training and no longer only the office manager. Well . . . It's not really my title yet, but that is what I like to call myself. I have to get my PI license first to be official. I'm taking an online class and should be finished in three months. I've already assisted with twenty cases. Right now, he has me working on three cases, and investigation is definitely my thang. Being an amateur snoop all these years has paid off. I know what to look for, and with access to all of these new databases at the agency, I'm just as good as *Monk* or the *Law and Order* team.

I even have a few of my friends that chip in and help me dig deeper. My girl, Maddy Lewis, a divorce attorney in NYC, is a super sleuth. And my old college roommate, Deborah Leonti, works in bank fraud investigation in L.A. She loves helping me out. I used them to research dudes I met online to see if their stories matched up. They don't play. With a touch of a button, they could tell me a guy's age, since a lot of dudes lie. I could find out who lives in the house with him, how many kids he has, what lawsuits have been filed against him, and if he's ever been to jail—mind-blowing shit. Most times, it was way more info than I wanted. I just wanted to make sure they weren't serial killers—but I guess my girls love finding liars too. Sick hobby, some might say, but I think it saves a lot of people years of trouble.

I started filing reports and sending follow-ups to new inquiries who contacted us through our website. It was the most tedious part of my job, but it was the main reason I was hired. They needed admin help badly. My cell vibrated on my desk.

Antonio: Ky, I need your help on a job. You free?
Kylie: Tonight? Still in office.
Antonio: Yeah. Tonight. Can you be ready in a couple of hours? You gotta dress up a bit.

I fluffed up my 'fro, which was looking good today, but then I glanced down at my faded jeans, sandals, and teal crocheted tank top. Not quite dressy. I called him.

His deep raspy voice answered, sounding amped up. "What up, Ky? You down?"

"Hey, Antonio. What do you mean by dress up? What is it?"

"I need to do some surveillance, but it's a date-night kinda spot . . . so to speak. You gotta look sexy. Can you pretend to be my date?"

I grinned. "Oh, really? You sure this is work? Don't try to make me your arm candy now," I said jokingly.

"Don't flatter yourself. You fine and all, but you told me you want to stay platonic, so I'ma obey your wishes . . . for now." He sarcastically cleared his throat.

"So, what do you mean, dress up? I'm in jeans. I gotta go home?" I sighed, not really feeling in the mood to get cute and put on makeup. I wanted to take off my bra, throw on my fluffy slippers, a tank top, and my Columbia University jogging shorts.

Antonio reassured me, "You got a li'l time. We gotta be there around 9:00 to 9:30 p.m., at the latest. Just put on a simple black dress. You know? Like if we were going to South Beach for dinner or something. Don't all you women have a little black dress?"

"Yes, we do," I laughed. "What job is this anyway?" I looked at the schedule on the whiteboard. "I don't have you out there doing any jobs this late."

"Ah, it's a side thing. Can a Black man make his little money? My homie is paying me. I'll come scoop you from your house around 8:30. It'll be fun. You need the training anyhow. Don't worry; I'll break you off a little something," he laughed.

"Huh? 'cuse me?" I rolled my neck as if he could see me.

"Money . . . I'll break you off a little money for coming with me. Cash. Get your dirty head out of the gutter, Kylie," he shouted.

"Okay, cool. I can use the extra cash. My poor little Beetle needs car service."

"Okay, see you soon," Antonio said.

This should be fun—a play date with my fine coworker, Antonio.

I rushed home and found a cute little dress to put on. It stopped just above the knees and had a scoop neck to show off "the girls." I put my hair in an updo roll with a funky Afro puff in the front.

As I was getting ready, I was blasting a sexy Yahzarah album, and my ringer wasn't even on, but just like clockwork, something told me to look at my phone on the bed. We were always in sync. Breeze's photo popped up on my cell with his sexy grin and bedroom eyes. It was my favorite photo of him rocking a NY Yankee's baseball cap and a white tee . . . pure New York swag. Made my knees weak every time he called, and I saw it.

I put him on speaker.

"Heeeey, Breeze."

"Hey, Ky . . . Hang up. Meant to FaceTime you."

"Uhhh, I can't. I have you on speaker. Getting dressed."

"Where you going?"

"Out," I giggled.

"Oh, I see. It's a Sunday night, and you got the music pumping. Where the party at?"

"Hold up, let me find out. Are you my dad now? It's not really a party. It's work."

"Soooo?"

"So . . . what?" I laughed as I fluffed up the front of my hair and smoothed out the sides.

"Is it a date?"

"Breeeze, stop tripping. Why you acting all jealous? It *is* work. Antonio and I doing surveillance. It's not a real date. He's my coworker." I put on my red matte lipstick.

"Yeah, a'ight . . . You think he don't want some of that sweet nectar you got?"

I smiled, knowing he was right. I chuckled. "It's work, Breeze. I really love what I'm doing now. It's a lot of fun catching the bad guys."

"You always did think you were Columbo. I am proud of you, darling."

"Ah, thanks, babe."

"I'm serious. Get reeeeally good, so you can open up a branch in NYC for them. Like a Fly on the Wall, Harlem, USA. Y'all would make a killing. Tracking down baby daddies who owe money and shit."

We laughed.

I yelled, "You are soooo stupid."

"Jokes aside, we gotta figure out a plan to have you doing what you love . . . but here, next to me. In New York."

I turned the music down and took a deep breath. I sighed as if I didn't believe him, but I really was feeling good that he kept pushing the issue. Maybe he wasn't just pulling my chain this time.

He continued, "I'm straight now: steady income, savings. I got a sexy three-bedroom in Westchester. We can get this family started. Plant these seeds for real this time," he chuckled.

I sat down on the bed and turned off the music completely. My stomach did a flip. "Breeze, don't play like that."

"Suga, I'm not playing. Ain't no need. You already know what it is. Like you know who is really here for you. You want to be a detective. I support you 110 percent . . . just as long as you can support my dreams as well."

I said nothing. I'd held on for more than ten years to the "I'm not ready yet" bullshit. But I heard sincerity in his voice this time. Maybe all those years of being a player caught up with him, and he was just tired. Maybe he really saw I was a woman now and not his little plaything.

"Hang up, Ky. I wanna see your face. I wanna see you."

He could sense I was in deep thought from my silence. I wanted to see him too. I wanted to make sure his eyes weren't lying. I took a deep breath. "Okaaaay."

I hung up, and he called me back right away on FaceTime. He was sitting on his couch. Gray tank top, fresh haircut, smooth mustache and goatee, biceps poppin', looking deliciously chocolate, and smiling ear to ear.

"There's my suga. Look at yoooou. Looking all fine and shiiiit." He pointed a finger at the screen with a raised eyebrow. "This *better* be work."

I laughed. "Breeze, 'we' aren't there yet, so stop regulating like a warden."

"You know you always gonna be my woman. Seriously. I was always real with you. I was honest. I wasn't ready. We were young. I had a lot on my plate with my family drama and all. I just—"

"Let's be clear. You *weren't* always honest, and you left out a lot of details. You let me know what you wanted me to know, and that's what really hurt me, Breeze. I always had to hear stuff through the grapevine."

His forehead creased in anger. "What you want me to do? Run down a list of side chicks I was fuckin' over the past ten years? Come on. Let's be real. You want to know just as much as I want to know niggas you been kicking it with. Look, if we're gonna be honest, my real issue was those abortions you had. I was holding a lot of resentment. But I love you, Kylie. I wanna see if we can try again . . . if we can make it work. Just you and me—no outside interference." His eyes looked so full of hope as he awaited my response.

"I . . . I have a new life here in Miami. I'm just beginning to make new friends and learn the ropes here. You know we are like family. You are a part of who I am now, but I just gotta see how it could work."

"Well, I was saving this for later, but FaceTime will have to do. I got a major publishing deal with Sony Music. Zane Taylor also hired me to produce his next album. It's serious money, Ky. Serious as in, you will be straight. You don't even have to work if you don't want to. But I know you." He shook his head and smiled.

I jumped up. "Sony . . . Zane Taylor . . . Breeeeze, that's amazing. You are going to be like the next P. Diddy, Babyface, Missy Elliott, Teddy Riley, or Timberlaaa—"

"Easy, baby, not rich yet, but we will be good for a while. A long while. These gigs are getting me more known and more connected."

My mind flashed on video hoes in the studio. Long nights at clubs. Gold diggers. Travel. Strippers and hoes. Singers who have to do the track over and over and over. Rappers and their groupies. My jealousy boiled, and I just had to sit back down.

"What's with you?"

"It just that . . . that lifestyle." I felt a lump in my throat. "That music industry world. I just don't like it. I don't want to be around it." I really meant to say I didn't want *him* around it.

"And you don't have to, give or take a few events I need you to come with me to. You know I gotta show you off, suga."

My head was spinning from flashbacks of all of the drama in my college years. Late-night partying, then showing up on my doorstep drunk, with a cloud of weed over his head and wanting to get "some."

"Let's just keep talking, 'cause now I don't know what to do."

He looked closely at the phone. "Do the right thing." He licked his lips and winked. "You know what I would do to you if I were right there?"

"What?" I tilted my head into the camera and smiled.

"I woulda bent you over that dresser and pulled that dress up and pounded you deep from the back. Pull your hair and—"

"Damn, Breeze, why you like torturing me?"

Above his head in the screen I saw a chat bubble pop up. Antonio texted me, "OMW."

I smoothed out my dress and checked myself in the mirror. "I gotta finish getting ready."

"All right, be safe and tell that nigga I *said*, don't try nothing. Keep it professional." The intensity in his glare was penetrating. And as much as I hated to admit it, even his jealously was a turn-on. He never went overboard with it. I just like knowing that he cared.

"Yes, daaaaddy," I said playfully. I blew a kiss into the phone. "Ciao, baby."

"Let's finish this conversation later. How long you gonna be out?"

"I should be done in a few hours. I do want to finish this." I smiled innocently at the phone.

"A'ight, suga. Call me whenever. I'll be here. Peace."

Is the fantasy I've had all these years about Breeze and me finally coming true? I might have to admit that maybe all this time, *I'm* the one with the commitment issues since I'm not sure this time around.

Chapter 6

Jacques

I was more than nervous, but I figured if I looked good, it would help soften Vicky's attitude. I had a fresh shave and haircut, plus I put on the black, button-down shirt she bought me last year. She said I looked good in black. Yes, I was trying hard to impress her. Being sentimental might just work too.

I wondered if she missed me as much as I did her. Big Pink was our favorite lunch spot on South Beach. I fumbled with the silver ring on my thumb and stared at the birds bathing in the water fountain while waiting for her.

First, I felt her energy: a rush of goose bumps formed on my forearms and in my scalp. Then I heard her walking close. I knew her strong New York strut. *Clickity clackity, clickity clackity.* She was a little late, but not too much. I broke my stare at the birds and saw pink stilettos in front of me, and then I glanced up with a smile. My throat tightened as I rose up. My stomach trembled. I felt like it was our first date.

"Heeeey, Vicky. Wow, look at you." Her sensual scent took me in. I took an exaggerated whiff of the air. "The Bvlgari perfume I got you?" I opened my arms to hug her. She nodded yes and hugged me back tighter than I expected.

Her cushiony pink lips shined with a light gloss. "Hi, Jacques. Thank you for the flattery."

"No, seriously, you look great, Vic. I mean, you've been working out more or something?" Her muscular calves teased me in her purple and pink strapless dress that hugged her at the hips and gave me just a peek of cleavage. Vicky was the master of seduction. If she planned to torture me, it was working.

We sat down, and I tried to compose myself. It was hard not to gawk at her. I really missed her.

Her voice was warm and soothing. "You look good too, you know." She moved her long mink like black hair. It fell like big waves over to one shoulder. I wanted to run my fingers through it so badly. I wanted to kiss her.

"You know this is hard . . . for both of us, Jacques. I mean, everything that happened between us . . . It was just so fast how it came crashing down. We were together for two years. I just know we can at least remain friends."

Friends? I swallowed and plastered a pleasant smile on my face. "Absolutely . . . but I would like more. Friends is a good start, though. I know maybe you needed to cool down, so I could explain more of the misunderstandi—"

"Jacques, I don't need to go into the past. I don't need the details. I just want to be friends, not enemies." She flipped through a menu nervously. I don't know why since she gets the same sandwich every time.

"You want me to order for you?"

"Sure."

"Your regular tuna with spinach wrap?"

"Yes," she blushed.

I wanted to get up and walk over to the counter to get our waiter. I wanted to do anything to get us off of this "friends" nonsense. Friends? I can't be friends with her. She moved from New York to be with me. She got a job at the Miami Police Department as a detective to be close to me. Yes, I know I fucked up. But I could make it up to her. As far as she knows, I only kissed Dee.

The waiter brought the sandwiches to our table, and we ate slowly with less chatter than usual. I was on edge, trying to get through it. I listened to her give me updates on her life, but all I could think about was how cold this meeting felt. She used to hold my hand . . . touch my face. Very affectionate. While I was driving, she'd massage my neck and talk to me. This was odd. It felt like we were coworkers. Or friends. I hated it.

I tried to fill the dead space. "So, what's new on the job? Solve any cases lately?"

"Oh yes, one of the biggest ones yet. It was all over the news last week. We caught a couple that had been trafficking teenage girls. They were using their Miami modern dance school as a front. Two girls were found dead in a trailer twelve years ago in Nevada. But thank God, the third one got away and was able to tell the cops it was her dance instructor and boyfriend. They held her captive as a sex slave for days. Her parents thought she was at a national dance contest. Poor thing was only 15. Word on the street is they were just a fraction of the large pedophile sex ring being discovered in Miami and Fort Lauderdale. Can you believe that shit?"

"Disgusting. They're going to get serious payback in prison. You know the laws of Karma."

"Oh, you better believe it. They will never see daylight— fucking demons. We still have to track where they were for the last twelve years and see if there are any other victims. The FBI is on the case now, though, with us. We're going to find the rest of them."

"Congrats. Sounds like a huge win."

"Thanks."

My stomach lurched, and I felt tightness in my neck.

"The guy is gonna take the easy way out." I saw a vision of him hanging himself in his cell.

"Suicide, you think?"

"Yes, soon. He won't make it six months."

"We'll have to make sure that doesn't happen. I'll tell my team to spread the word and put his ass on suicide watch. He needs to rot in jail." She perked up and showed me all of her perfectly white teeth. "Thanks, Papi . . . I mean, Jacques. I miss you helping with my cases with them intuitive abilities you got."

"You can still call me Papi . . . even if we're friends. And, you know, I will always help you." I softly touched the top of her thigh.

"Come on. Stop." She smiled and then forced a serious face. This was such an act. I could see her aura glowing with love and desire. I know she missed me. I could also feel her pain of betrayal.

I took a deep breath to release it. It was too much to take in.

"Vicky, dammit, I miss you. Can you please come back home? I'm so sorry I lost your trust, but I didn't sleep with her. I didn't have sex. I know I was wrong but—"

She looked into my eyes. Hers shined like copper coins. She bit her bottom lip and mumbled. "Jacques . . . I met someone."

My spoon dropped into my soup bowl. "Huh?"

"I . . . I met someone. It's not too serious, but I'm dating again. I missed you like crazy, but I realized that maybe it's best we stay friends. I was so angry and hurt. Even when I think about coming back, I know it's going to be hard to trust you. You have women clients that want you everywhere. I never, ever thought you would be the one to let your desires get a hold of you. I did everything I could to keep you satisfied, and that wasn't enough."

"No, no, Vicky, please stop." I put my hand on her wrist.

"I was probably putting too much pressure on you to have a family. I mean, I get it from my mom, my abuela, my sisters. I'm 34 and not getting any younger. My family says I am getting too caught up in work that I'm going to let my childbearing years pass me by."

"You're fine, Vic. You are nowhere near menopause."

"I wanted nothing more than to have my little Puerto Rican, Moroccan, French babies with you." She laughed. My eyes started to water. "So, when all that shit came to light on your birthday, it just turned my world upside down." Her chest heaved as if she were holding back a cry.

"We can still have our babies. I want you in my life." My voice cracked as I lied. "I'm ready for a family, Vicky."

"Papi, I love you, and I always will, but be honest . . . if I wanted to have a baby right now, would you? It's been two years, and you would freak out at just the mention of me getting pregnant."

"Noooo, no . . . That's not true. So much has happened in the last few months alone. My mom passing, my brother acting up, losing you. It made me rethink a lot of things."

I wanted to believe it myself.

"I don't even want to feel like I'm giving you an ultimatum or that I stole your freedom. Or worse, we get married and have kids, and you cheat on me because deep down, you really weren't ready."

"I wouldn't do that." I clenched my jaws because now, I was angry that she seemed to have already made up her mind.

"All I'm saying is I don't hate you, and now you can have a little fun without guilt, and I'll do the same." Just then, I felt a giant knife plunge into my heart and turn slowly.

Vicky got a text and looked at it with a smile. She replied as the knife continued to turn and turn in my chest, even slower. I tapped my foot to distract myself from the pain.

She put her phone down and continued. "If we are really meant to be, then I guess it would happen eventually. I just think nothing is a coincidence." She sighed. "Well, I feel good now that I got that off my chest." The knife pulled out and went back in harder for another round. "There is a lesson in all of this . . . for both of us."

I shook my head. She fucked him. I know whoever it was, he is fucking her good. I held back tears and cleared my throat. I had nothing more to say. I felt like an ass thinking she was probably meeting with me to reconcile. I was pouring my heart out, and she was just really here to gloat.

She looked at her phone. "Well, it's 6:30 p.m. I gotta run." She delicately wiped her mouth with her napkin and slowly reapplied her lip gloss as she looked at me. Her soft lips puckered and rubbed together.

"Why so soon? Where are you going?" I clenched my jaws, mad at myself for letting that escape my desperate and pathetic mouth. I was not her man anymore. She had made that clear.

She tilted her head to the side as if I had no right to ask. "Oh, out with the girls. It's Taylor's party . . . you know, from yoga? A divorce party."

"So sorry to hear that."

"No, no, she's happy. It's a celebration."

As I pictured Taylor's smiling face, I suddenly felt all of her chakras shut down, and I felt pushed into a wall. I felt afraid. "Was he, was he a bully or something? Abusive?"

"Damn, you are always on point with your shit. Yeah, emotionally and physically. He was a monster, so it's really a good thing she's finally freeee." She stood up.

I joined her. "Well . . ."

She pulled her hair up over her shoulders and let it fall down her back. I stood in front of her and rested my hands on her shoulders.

"You are so beautiful. Why don't you come over tonight after the party?" I leaned in and grabbed her chin closer to my face, just an inch apart from my mouth. She tapped my hand gently for me to let go.

"Jacques . . . friends."

Bile and dread inched up slowly in my throat.

"Okay, I will respect your wishes." I shrugged my shoulders and hugged her one last time. I held her tight as if it would be the last time I saw her. I rested my chin on her shoulder and smoothed out her hair. I missed touching her. I felt her body melting into mine. I knew she wanted me just as much as I did her.

I whispered in her ear, "Tonight, Vic. I never changed the locks."

She sighed as if contemplating it. "We'll see." She let down her guard and pecked me on the lips.

Well, that wasn't a no. She quickly walked away with an extra swivel in her hips. She wanted me to see what I had been missing. God, she had such a nice ass. I shouted, "Have fun, but not toooo much fun."

She turned around and waved me off with a laugh.

I ordered a beer and sat down to watch the birds some more. I couldn't believe she was going to a party now. There would probably be strippers or just a lot of single men preying on women like her. I felt she definitely had slept with someone. That pep in her stride told me she'd spread her legs for someone else, and I hated it. I'd never been jealous, but I was now fuming.

I'm seeing someone. That was going to play over and over in my head.

Yes, I finally had sex with Dee, so I guess we're even now. Honestly, if I found out that she messed around behind my back, even a kiss . . . I probably wouldn't be as kind as her. Women are indeed troopers at forgiving infidelity, where men will usually hate you for life and call you every slut and whore in the book. What most men don't realize is that even if a woman forgives you, she will get revenge in some way, shape, or form. It's almost a 100 percent guarantee. I see it every day in my readings. They might call me to find out about their husband of fifteen years, but they also have two boyfriends on the side.

Vicky wanting to be friends told me she hadn't crossed all the way over to the other side of the fence. The grass is not greener, and she knew it. She wanted to keep that door cracked with me. I felt good by knowing she didn't hate me, and she still wanted to be in my life. She was probably not coming tonight, I decided, but I prayed that she would. I was not giving up on us.

As I walked away from the Big Pink Restaurant feeling sorry for myself, my cell rang, and I was happy to see Dee's name appear.

"Jacques, oh my God, you were so right about me getting my new business off the ground."

"That's great. What happened?"

"Okay, so, remember in my reading you gave me when I was in Miami? You said you saw me launching my own business. Well, one of my former clients who—by the way, is a filthy rich computer mogul—he-he offered to be an angel investor, and he wants me to broker deals with some of his computer programs."

"Wow. That was no coincidence. Congratulations."

"He wants me to work for him first as a consultant so that his team can train me on his products, but technically, he will be my first client. Aaaand, you also told me I would start my own boutique firm in nine months or less."

"I did?"

"Yes. Jacques, my feelings be hurt when you don't remember half the amazing shit you tell me."

"Dee, come on. It's not you. I usually don't remember the details of readings. Do you know I speak to so many people in a week? All of their stories start blending in together, and it's just overwhelming to remember them all. If I did . . . it wouldn't be good." I grinned and shook my head.

"Yeah, I'm sure you would be in a straitjacket by now."

"Meditation saves me, Dee. It really does. You have no idea."

"Maybe I'll do it one day," she teased since she knows that is one of her homework assignments to improve her life that I always give her. "Well, I know you like to get updates, and I just wanted to hear your sexy-ass accent. I cannot tell a lie."

"Aw, you are too kind."

"I'm gonna be back in your neck of the woods soon to check out some locations. I'll start small for an office."

I remembered there were some vacant offices in my building, but I knew better. That would be a disaster waiting to happen. I couldn't have Dee that close to me every day.

"You know what I was thinking? Maybe when I get a reading again in person, we can delve into that past life we had together. I want to know what happened to Saasha."

"Sounds like a plan. We definitely must celebrate your new business when you're back."

Her voice got softer and sultry. "Ooooh, you know that is *definitely* happening again. Talk to you soon." She whispered, "I miss that psychic dick too."

"Oh yeah? He heard you. He just jumped a little," I chuckled.

"You stuuuupid."

We cracked up. "All right, love, we'll talk soon."

"Bye, Jacques."

Chapter 7

Kylie

I was waiting on Antonio to pick me up, and the memories of Breeze kept resurfacing. He knows seeing him on FaceTime makes me feel closer to him and harder to forget. The sound of his voice and that look in his eyes always made a shift in me. One of my favorite quotes by Frida Kahlo was, "Take a lover that looks at you as if you are magic." That is the one thing I can't forget: how Breeze looks at me. It's like he adores me. As tough as he pretends to be, I do feel a deep connection with him since he shared secrets with me that many would never know. He let down his guard with me. Even though we've had our moments in the last ten years, I was considering my next steps more seriously. Especially since, deep down, I knew who he really was.

I was about 19, one night in my Columbia University dorm room, complaining about my mom to Breeze, who was lying stretched out on my bed looking at a basketball game while I did homework at my desk.

"Would you believe True used some of my student loan money without asking me? We have a shared account. I'm so fucking pissed. When I asked her why, she goes, 'I'll put it back in two weeks.' She needed to pay a deposit for a cruise. Reeeeally, a *cruise?*"

He took off his Yankee baseball cap and scratched his head. "Well, suga, a cruise is better than heroin. That's what my mom would have definitely used it on."

I dropped my pen. "What? Are you serious?"

"As a heart attack. She's been on and off drugs since I was 13." He shrugged his shoulders like it was no big deal. I suddenly felt horrible for complaining about my mom. I had no idea. He never really talked about his mother much. I knew they didn't get along, and his grandma raised him, but I never knew the whole story. I think his fear of abandonment and mommy issues is what always caused him to flee and not be in a commitment with me.

That night, he told me that it started with weed, moved to coke, crack, then heroin. She graduated from the school of drugs, so to speak. I finally understood why he acted like he was 42 when he was only 22. He had to grow up fast. He had to clean up her messes a lot.

"One time, my brother and little sister had to get her from a pool hall. They said she was giving head in the bathroom for five dollars. I didn't want to believe it, but one of my boys told me he saw her. We had to drag her out of there. I was fucking destroyed after that. I couldn't stand seeing her like that—hoeing for drugs.

"My dad had left a few years before and moved to Virginia. He'd send money, and she would spend everything we had—everything. Some nights, we didn't have dinner. You can't even sleep at night when you got a drug addict around ready to take what they can for their next high. I had to learn how to hustle early to make a little bread DJ'ing just to keep the rent paid."

"Oh, Breeeeze, I'm soooo sorry. Is she still on it?"

"Nah, she cleaned up a bit, but she still a mess. Think she just a drunk now. Her mind ain't the same. It's like mush. She has no reasoning. It's like she thinks she's a teenager. She's invincible. She's really bad with responsibility."

After opening up to me that night, he never talked much about her again.

***

I heard a car horn blow lightly and looked out the window. Antonio was already in the driveway. I quickly made sure the kitchen was clean and turned off all the lights so my roommate wouldn't lose it. Then I rushed out.

Antonio and I walked up to the door, and it was a single entrance in the alley. No name or address. If you were here, you had to be "in the know." I thought 9:00 p.m. was kind of early for a South Beach party, but I figured if Antonio needed me as a prop, I could help him out and see him in action.

He looked at me and smiled as he opened up his top button. "Just be cool. You're my old lady for tonight." He winked.

I felt the fall chill on my bare legs. It was 65 degrees, but that was chilly for Miami.

"Really? Your old lady?" I laughed. "You sound like you're 70."

"Okay, my lady. You're gonna enjoy this job."

"Why did we have to leave our cells in the glove compartment?"

"They aren't allowed. Lots of high-profile people here."

I was at a cross between nervous and excited. Then I heard "Fantasy" playing from an upstairs balcony. "Yessss, I love this song. It's so sexy, and the chords are sick. Has an old-school R&B feel. It's from Alina and Galimatias."

"Galima—who?"

"Oh, never mind." My useless music trivia is never appreciated.

Antonio rang the buzzer and shook his head. A deep baritone voice said through the intercom, "Yes, how can I help you?"

"Returning member and guest."

The door buzzer went off, and in we went. He held my hand and spoke softly, "Cameras are on us. Come on. Play your part, woman." We went into the elevator.

"Remember, I'm Will—"

"Oh, oh . . . Can I be Jada?" I teased.

"Ky, come on. This is serious business. Nah, you are Nia. I always had a thing for Nia Long." He squeezed my hand, indicating it was action time. The elevator doors opened to the penthouse. The music was pumping even louder, and that sexy song embraced us. This was exciting.

An elegantly dressed hostess greeted us. She had on stilettos and a long black dress with a high split. Blond with thin, short hair. Lips and cheeks pumped up with Botox and that extra shine they usually have on their cheeks. *Welcome to Miami*.

"Hello, Wayne?"

"Will," Antonio corrected her.

She had a strong Russian accent. "Ah, yes, Will. Nice to see you back."

She reached in for air kisses on the cheek and rubbed his shoulder. A bit too familiar if you ask me. *Helloooo . . . I'm his girl tonight. Do you not see me standing here, beeyotch?*

"And who is this beautiful one you bring?" She reached out her hand to pull me in for a hug. I wasn't ready for all the touchy-feely stuff and didn't embrace her as much as she did me.

"Oh, I don't bite, honey. I'm Bianca. You are?"

Antonio answered for me. "Nia." He put his hand over my shoulder, "Nia, my new girlfriend."

"Oh . . . You are a lucky girl, Nia." She licked her lips and smiled like she knew something I didn't.

He interrupted her flirting. "I paid online for her." She snapped back into reality and looked on the computer screen in front of her on the podium. "Which room will you be in?"

"Not sure. Tonight, we'll probably just walk around. First time." He nodded his chin toward me.

A dance floor was in the background, with a few couples dancing. Definitely not a poppin' club. Then I looked to my right and saw a couple making out while a woman was giving a lap dance to her man. As my eyes wandered, I was startled as Bianca rubbed the curve in my waist and slid her hand down to rest on my ass.

"You are beautiful, Nia. I love your hair. I will look for you later, 'kay?"

I was shocked, and I felt violated, but I nodded politely, not to draw attention and stay in character.

As we walked away, I said, "Where in the hell did you bring me, Antonio? Is this a strip club, some type of sex playhouse?" I said through my teeth with a smile in case someone saw. "I'm gonna kill you."

He put his arm around me. "Relax, relaaaax. I'm looking for someone. One of my homies hired me to see if his wife was still coming here. Just chill . . . I won't let nothing happen to you. We're just observing. You might like it. I know you got a bit of freak in you on the low."

I sucked my teeth. The Jamaican in me surfaced when I was annoyed.

We walked down a long corridor with disco lights and passed a game room with two pool tables. There was an entrance to the locker room. How strange. A locker room in a club? Bowls of condoms, peppermints, and even lube were on a few counters. Two big screens were on with porno playing and on mute.

"What's behind there?" I asked him.

"Oh, you only wear a towel beyond that point."

I put up a stop sign with my hand. "Say no more. We *won't* be going that way."

"Nah, Ky, you good." The music was getting louder, and now it switched to techno.

Then I heard it. Sighs. Deep sighs of ecstasy. I thought it was the music. But I looked to my right, and through the glass, all I saw were naked bodies with a black light over them. They were on what looked like a giant bed, but more like king-size beds pushed together. The energy was intense and rapid. I saw legs, butts, arms, tongues, breasts—all different shades. A fire grew inside of me. The moaning, the sucking, and groaning were seeping through the walls. The smells were strong too. Lingering of latex and sex. It was like someone sprayed pheromones in the air.

The glass was slightly steamy from the other side, and then one girl pressed up against it as someone grabbed her hips from behind. I saw the sheets being clenched for dear life. Her face was full of pleasure as her partner entered her. I was frozen and yet very, *very* turned on. I looked at Antonio. "Antonio, really? This is a swinger's club?" I already knew the answer.

He smiled and pointed to the black leather bench in the corner. "Have a seat and enjoy the view. I'm looking for this redheaded chick. If you see one, let me know." He showed me a small photo he had in his pocket of her. She was cute and looked like an innocent schoolteacher. It's always the ones you least suspect.

He seemed totally unmoved by the massive orgy happening right before our eyes on like ten beds pushed together. Unreal. He was calm as if I had a rerun of *American Idol* on in front of him.

I sat up straight and crossed my legs. He sat down next to me and rubbed my thigh. "Relax . . . You're with me. I had to come with a date." He raised his eyebrows. "Keeps me out of trouble."

I wondered what trouble he had already been in here. The way the hostess was drooling over him, I'd say plenty. "Oh-oh, I think I see her." He got closer to the glass and left me in the dark corner.

An older white man sat next to me—handsome, salt-and-pepper goatee. Solid build. Dressed in black slacks and white top with a few buttons opened.

"First time?"

I looked at him, but he stared ahead. "Yes." I stared blankly back at the glass room of sinful lust. It was so hard to turn away. I gulped as two women made out with a man, and he fingered them both simultaneously. Now, *that* was talent.

I shifted in my seat.

"Oh, you'll warm up soon. When you are ready . . . Look at me." His hand tapped my shoulder. I flinched.

He chuckled at my nervousness. "That's my wife you're watching." He pointed to the woman whose face was pressed up against the glass with her mouth open. "It's her birthday. I like to watch. If you like what you see, maybeeee we can have some fun later? I have a private room here." He shrugged his shoulders with a hopeful look in his eyes.

"No, noooo . . . I don't think so."

Antonio came back just in time. "Oh, Alejandro, right? What's up, my dude?"

"Will. What's going on, brother? I didn't know this was *your* woman. Niiiice." As if I weren't sitting right there . . .

"Yeah, this is Nia. She's all mine . . . for now." He winked at me.

"Yeah, sharing helps the relationship last longer." He looked at me and smiled. Alejandro turned to Antonio and said, "Do you think you up for the Purple Haze Room in like thirty? I reserved it."

"Nah, not tonight. Just showing her around. You seen Rubia? I thought I saw her."

"Yeah, she is here a lot, but not with her husband. Usually on weekends. Haven't seen her tonight . . . You tried that yet? She is *wild*." He turned to me and waved his hand. "Oh, no disrespect."

I shrugged.

Antonio scratched the back of his head, ignoring the question. "I . . . I thought I saw her."

Alejandro shook his head and pointed proudly, "Nope, she's not in there, but Soledad is."

Antonio turned around to the glass, and his wife was now on her back with two men on top of her doing some things I never saw even in a porno. These people were beyond freaky. Antonio seemed to get a kick out of my reaction, and I was trying to act calm, like this was normal. As if seeing ten people fuck and suck right before my eyes was just a regular Sunday night for me. But my facial expressions always gave me away. I know I probably looked like a deer caught in headlights.

The music switched to reggae, and Antonio started swaying a bit and came over to me with his hand out to get up and join him. I forgot I was "his girl" tonight, so I had to play along. My shoulders were tight. I was so guarded.

He pulled me close and spoke softly in my ear. "Loosen up, Ky. You got this look on your face like you been kidnapped." He swayed his hips into mine and held the small of my back. I had no idea he had moves like that. I looked up into his eyes. He sure was sexy, but wilder than I knew.

I smiled, trying to play it off since Alejandro and a few others were watching us. I whispered back, "Well, you told me we were doing surveillance and that it was a party. How could you leave out that it was a fucking sex club? How do you want me to react?"

"Yeah, like if I told you . . . you would come." He did a little dip down to his knees and slid his hands on my waist as he came up.

I smiled and shook my head.

"Plus, I got some free feels out of this gig. Made it all worth it." He laughed and looked around one last time. "Well, I don't see Rubia." He danced close to me and held my chin. "Do you want to stay and watch?"

A Black couple walked by us and smiled. The woman, looking dead at Antonio's crotch, said, "Hello. You guys wanna play?" He looked her up and down. Skintight black tube top and skirt. Boob job. Enormous hips and ass. Nice weave, but she looked tired in her face, like she'd had a hard life.

Her man, who wasn't bad looking, smiled at me and mouthed, "Come on." Like he knew me, and it was for old time's sake. He had on no shirt and was very buff—the gross kind, where their arms don't touch their sides. *I'll pass on you, Mr. Stranger Danger.*

Antonio said, "No, thanks, we were just leaving, but maybe next time?"

I jumped in and said in a flirty tone, "Yes, *definitely* next time" and smiled at them both. Antonio looked at me in shock and had a little smirk on his face.

I said softly, "What? I was just playing along." I shrugged my shoulders.

He squeezed my hand as if to say shut up. They waved goodbye and continued on their search for another conquest.

The room behind the glass changed to flashing blue lights, and it was so hard to turn away. These people had no inhibitions at all. They weren't all models either. Some a bit heavy and out of shape, stretch marks, thigh dimples . . . all that. Yet, some were very beautiful, like they lived in the gym or had outstanding surgeons.

Overall, this gig was worth it since I think I learned a few new tricks from just watching.

He held my hand about to walk out. I didn't move. "Can they see us?"

"No, the mirror is one-sided. They just see themselves."

"Wow. That must be a serious turn-on, knowing people are watching you . . . but not knowing who."

"Oh yeah . . . It's definitely an experience." He stood behind me now, and we were just swaying to the music watching. It felt weird and yet good being in his arms.

"Really?" I laughed, "You seem like a pro . . . They seem to know 'Will' around these parts. You know what took me by surprise? I thought everyone in here would look like South Beach models or porn stars."

"Nah, but sometimes, it is the nerdy secretary or neglected housewife that will turn that ass out . . . They've been holding in a lot of shit. Pent-up frustrations, and here is where they can be themselves." He was pressing up against me more than he needed to, and I didn't stop him. I felt his hardness. I was getting warm. Shit.

I looked behind my shoulder at him. "Oh, is that what happened to you, Will? You got turned out?"

"Nah, never that. I'm just saying the people you least expect got a lot of freak in them." His hands ran down the sides of my waist. He held me from the front, wrapping his hands across my stomach. He spoke in my ear, and I tingled from the heat from his breath. "You know what I'm talking about, right, Ky?"

Fuck. Hold it together, Kylie. Hold it together.

"Yeah . . . I do. I do. So . . . You aren't a regular?"

"No, this is just my third time. I came for work. I don't get sidetracked, but I did have a little fun last time. But I know I gotta stay on track. That's why you're here."

He slapped me on the ass. I jumped. "Let's go. Yeah . . . right on track. You are really getting into character."

I was enjoying "Will" and not feeling the pressure of us at work. I didn't want to leave.

Antonio whispered, "So, you never wanted to try something like this?"

He looked at the white woman on her knees, who was pleasuring a chocolate brother. This lucky fella had two women behind his back, caressing his back, butt, and each other.

I spoke slowly in his ear. "Well, in my mind, it seems like fun, but I would be scared. I don't want to bump into someone I know. And the diseases . . . aren't you afraid you might—"

"Well, you can't do it with everyone. And they have a strict policy here. No means no. No one will force themselves on you if you don't want it." He whispered, "I'd actually rather watch . . . Don't look now, but Rubia just entered. Act like we are just watching the room."

He buried his face in my neck and nibbled, then kissed it and lightly sucked it. I acted like I was pretending, but it felt *really* good. His big hands were clasping me so tight. My head sank into my left shoulder as he buried his face into my neck. Then I glanced and saw this petite lady with bright red hair . . . It was a bright Raggedy Ann red.

I kept swaying to the music, and it was a good excuse to grind up on Antonio. I looked back and said, "What is the whole story with her, anyway?"

"Well, she and her husband used to come together. She got a little jealous of some of the women and told him they should stop going. He agreed, but he had a feeling she was still coming on her own. He didn't have any proof, but he said if she's lying, he's done."

"Damn, she's grimy with it."

"Well, her man ain't no angel, so you know how that goes . . . a woman scorned."

"I don't see what was so exciting about her. She's cute but—"

"Well, word on the street has it that she is *very* skilled."

He stood in front of me. "Look, I'm sorry if I got a little carried away up in your neck, but damn, you smell good, guuuurl." He snapped out of character when he noticed Rubia move away. She smiled at us as she walked into the locker room to get out of her dress and into her towel. He tapped my waist. "I want to wait and see if she goes in there."

A few minutes went by as we danced to an '80s song to keep busy. He really was a smooth dancer with his tall self. I couldn't keep my eyes off of what was going on behind the glass, though. Rubia made her way to the middle of the giant bed, and a few men left the women who they were dealing with to try to get with her.

Antonio saw the curiosity in my eyes, and I said, "Isn't that her in the far left against the wall with those three people?"

"Damn, she didn't waste any time. That's *exactly* what I needed to see." He poked me in the side of my waist. "Look at you. You know you wanna go in there. You don't have to do anything. You can just watch." He tugged on my dress. "But you have to be naked. Butt-ass naked." He smiled and licked his lips.

I actually thought about it for a second, but I knew I couldn't do that.

"Nah, Antonio—not a good idea."

"I know, are you kidding me? Vince would kill me if I took advantage of his precious, Kylie."

"Took advantage? Pleeeease." If he only knew what I would do to him. I just rolled my eyes at him, and he laughed.

"Come on." He held my hand. "I think we got enough intel for my client. I'm gonna take you home before we get into trouble."

"For real." We held hands walking out casually as "Nia" and "Will."

Secretly, I hoped we'd return.

Antonio dropped me off at home, and we resumed our coworker relationship as if nothing just happened between us. I loved tall men . . . He had to be about six foot four, and he had beautiful chocolate skin like Breeze, but I knew trouble when I saw it, so I planned to stay clear and keep it professional. Breeze was enough to deal with as it was. When I got home, he reached out like clockwork.

Breeze: Home yet?
Kylie: Almost, just getting dropped off. I'll call you in a few.

When I got in, it was about 12:30 a.m. Mackenzie was there, but she was conked out with the TV on. Her door was shut, but I could hear her soft snores under the sounds of the show *Snapped*. She was obsessed with those marathons. How she fell asleep to women killing their husbands in the most brutal ways was amazing. She also interned in the ER at one point, so I guess nothing really fazed her. I love my crime shows, but I couldn't go to sleep with that on in the background. It was a nightmare waiting to happen.

I was still in awe of what happened at the swingers' club and not sure if I could tell Breeze even half of that story. No, I knew I couldn't tell him where I just came from. Who was I kidding? He'd freakin' lose it. I kicked off my heels in the hallway, took out the bobby pins in my hair that held my 'fro in an updo, and sat on the stool, taking in all that just happened. Soon, I strolled into the kitchen and poured myself a tall glass of water and walked into my bedroom as I called Breeze on FaceTime. He was lying in his bed watching TV. The blue screen illuminated off of his body. No shirt, only boxers and a smile. Just the way I liked him.

"Well, looks like you had a good time, suga."

"Why you say that?"

"Your makeup is worn off. Your hair. You look tired."

"I am. We just had to go to this whack-ass party and look for this redheaded chick who was cheating on her husband."

"You find her?"

"Yes sirrrr . . . We always do."

"Look at you, acting like you on the police force and shit."

"Shut up," I laughed. "You just nervous I'm learning new detective tricks."

"Please, you can look me up. I ain't got nothing to hide, suga. So . . . Can we just talk about our plans, or you too tired?"

"Okay, what plans?"

"As I said earlier, I want to do this with you for real."

"Well, I want someone I can trust, someone I feel at home with, someone who gets me, someone I love."

"What . . . I'm all that."

"I just get scared, Breeze."

"Scared of what, darling?"

"You've been on your own single all this time. It's hard to change just like that. I know you."

"Well, Kylie, we never really gave it a shot."

"I never knew you really wanted a shot. Let's be real, Breeze. You haven't been consistent. You flip-flop. It's only since I've moved to Miami that you been talking about locking me down."

"We don't communicate. Have you ever even actually asked me what has been going on with me lately? You always assuming. You keep me focused; you keep me grounded. I need you around." He sat up and looked closer into the screen. "When you are around, shit just goes right, Ky. Everything you said I would do with my business, with my production company has come true. This deal I got is because of you. You pushed me and believed in me when no one else did."

"Wow, really? So, I'm just your good luck charm or something?"

"Yeah, if you wanna be a smart-ass. A nigga over here pouring his heart out and you wanna . . ."

I rubbed my Afro and yawned.

He continued, "Yeah, we should talk tomorrow. You look tired. Go to bed, suga, and we'll talk tomorrow."

"I'm not tired."

"Yes, you are. And when you tired, you say snappy shit. I'ma call you in the morning, okay?" He moved the phone closer so that I could see his eyes. "I miss you, Ky."

"Miss you too. Night." I hung up feeling like I entered another dimension. I was trying to listen to him and really believe his bullshit, but I kept seeing flashes of butts, pink, brown, and pale penises, and all kinds of breasts pressed up on the glass. I kept hearing the sighs . . . the moaning. That shit was unreal. It was . . . pretty liberating, in fact. I wish I were that brave.

I had to take a shower to wash off those dirty thoughts. Even if I didn't believe his whole commitment promises, I knew he was definitely going to deliver on the penis soon.

Chapter 8

Kylie

My little blue Beetle was filled to the max after I got the remaining items I left in Mom's garage. After this final drop-off, I would be officially moved into my new digs at Mackenzie's. I felt independent and free again.

I shoved a big garbage bag full of winter coats in the backseat. I might just end up donating them anyway. I doubt that I would need them here, and I didn't plan on traveling up north in the winter . . . like nevaaa, evaaa again.

I was startled by a loud base thumping. I turned around and saw it was my mom pulling into the driveway in her new cherry-red Corvette that Basim bought her for her forty-fifth birthday. Her last car got too junkie looking, and activist bumper stickers covered it, but she managed only to put one on this car. It read:

If You're Gonna Ride My Ass
At Least Pull My Hair.

Gotta love my mother. She was blasting "If I Was Your Girlfriend" by Prince.

"Mom!" I waved for her to turn it off. "Stop causing a scene with that loud-ass music."

"What?" She cut the car off and shook her fluffy blond 'fro. "Take your panties out of a knot, Granny. I need my Prince on the road. He helps soothe my road rage. You know these people down here drive worse than in New York?"

"I know." I walked up to her and kissed her cheek.

Her tone softened. "Hey, baby. I see you all packed up." She raised her hands in the air like she was testifying in church. "Hallelujaaaah. Now I can walk around naked and do what I want."

"Whatever . . . like you care. I didn't stop you from walking around naked."

"Well, now, I can make noise when Basim and I—"

I held my ears. "La la la la. Stop it, Mommy. You're gross."

She was hysterically laughing now. She loved to piss me off with her oversharing self.

"Here, you want something to do?" She handed me two bags from the trunk as she walked in front of me with three Whole Food grocery bags. She sashayed down the walkway to the door. Her long, aqua, maxi dress almost covered her feet but hugged her hips tighter than usual.

"Mommy, when you get so much booty? What you doing? That squat challenge on Facebook?" I followed her into the house.

"Girl, hush up ya mouth. Where you think you get your hot body from? You know them little boys are still hitting on me?"

"Yeah, my butt is not *poppin'* like that," I giggled. Phantom came running to greet us. He rubbed up on both of our ankles with his soft fur and meowed softly.

"Hey, Phantom, wassup up? I'm gonna miss you." I picked him up and squeezed his chunky frame. "I wanna squeeze you till you pop."

Mom's forehead crinkled. "Don't say that. I hate when you say that."

"Jeez, just kidding. Relax. I swear you love that cat more than me."

She sucked her teeth and continued unpacking. I put the cat down, and his copper eyes twinkled like he knew

I was leaving. I started to unpack the bags I had on the counter.

"No, no, Kylie. Just leave it. Don't worry about me. Go to your new place and unpack."

"It's no big deal. I can help." I pulled out spinach, papaya, sea salt, maca powder, agave, and some vitamins. I looked at the bottle and then back at my mother.

Silence.

I put the bottle down gently.

"Kylie, I . . . I just found out. I was going to tell you."

"Wait, like—for real? You already are?" I stared at the bottle again to make sure I was reading it right.

Prenatal pills.

She walked toward me and jumped dramatically. "Surprise! You're gonna be a big sister."

I nodded. "Yep, I am surprised. This is just soooo unexpected. I'm 28, Mom. We're gonna be changing diapers now?" I whined. "There is such a biiiig gap in time. Do you realize how old you'll be when the kid is in high school—college even?" I sighed and then saw her frown. "I'm sorry, I'm happy for you, though. I am." I hugged her. "At least the baby will have a great dad and never have to worry about money. And maybe a new baby will keep you grounded and out of the streets."

She grabbed my chin and looked into my eyes. "I was gonna invite you to dinner with Basim and tell you, but I guess the universe had other plans. You know you will still be my baby."

I smiled . . . and then suddenly felt jealous, furious—betrayed even. I wanted to be happy, but I wasn't. "Aye, I need a drink."

I sat down at the counter, and like clockwork, she had the wine and glass ready as if I were at a bar.

"Have one for me too."

I poured a glass and took a sip. "Mom, you're 45. Are you *sure* you wanna do this?"

"What? Of course, I do. I'm 45. I'm not 60. Look at Halle Berry, Janet Jackson . . . They were older when—"

"But, Mom, they're celebrities with money. They can do whatever they wan—"

"Basim has no children, and he has money. His spa is doing great, and he's going to travel less to help me out with the baby. I might even get a nanny since it's been so long if I need help."

I raised my eyebrows.

She took a dramatic inhale and closed her eyes. "I know I was not a good mother to you. This is . . . This is my second chance to do it right, and I'm still trying to get it right with you, Kylie, you know?"

"It's okay," I shrugged.

She yelled, "I didn't even know I was pregnant. I thought I was just menopausal since my cycle has been weird for the last two years. But the doctor said I'm healthy, and I'm definitely pregnant. Hence, my Beyoncé/JLO ass." She chuckled a deep, throaty laugh and did a little twerk holding onto the counter.

"Seeee . . . I knew your butt wasn't that fat before." I pointed to it.

"Jealous?"

"Yes, definitely." We laughed. I hung out for only a few minutes more so I could get home and deal with the Mack truck that just hit me square in the face. What a night this was going to be.

I couldn't drive home fast enough. I stormed in so quickly, I didn't even unpack my car. The powerful slam of the door startled me, but it was my own doing, rushing in to escape anyone seeing me break down. Waves of anger were flowing through my veins. I felt my chest was tight, and my breath was short. I couldn't hold it in anymore and ran inside my room and just started crying into a pillow. I exploded with emotion. I needed to get it out. I felt like a little kid who just got in trouble and was holding in their wails. I wasn't even really sure why I was crying, but I knew I had to be quiet in case Mackenzie was studying.

How could she do this *now?* Are you freakin' kidding me? Have a baby *now?* I was just teaching her to act like a mom after years of her trying to be my big sister or best friend. Now, I have to share her with a brand-new baaaaby? A baby. Okay . . . Okay, I knew I sounded selfish, but this was too much to take in.

My chest throbbed as if I had hiccups. I sniffled, and then I heard a gentle knock on the door.

Mackenzie's voice was muffled behind the door. "Kylie, you okay, buttercup?"

"Yes, yes . . . I'm fine." I quickly wiped my eyes and sniffled, looking for a tissue to blow my nose in.

"You crying?"

Dammit. So embarrassing.

"I'm okay. I'm good."

"All righty. Well, I'm here if you need me."

I got up and opened the door. "Hey, come in." I plopped back on my bed. "I just found out my mom is pregnant."

"Wait . . . Whaaaat? *Your* mom? How is that poss . . . How old is she?"

"She's 45."

Mackenzie counted quickly on her fingers. "Wow, she had you young then."

"Yes, 16. I'm just in shock. It's been a very rocky relationship. I just recently started calling her mom this year."

"For real? What the heck did you call her before?"

"Her nickname, True. Her real name is Paulette, but I been calling her True since I was a kid. She was always trying to be my buddy. She wasn't really 100 percent present as a mom. She didn't want the responsibility, I guess."

Mackenzie sat on the edge of my bed. "Chile, mother-hood ain't for everybody."

"Well, we've been working on our relationship. It was getting a lot better. Especially when she revealed some heavy shit about my dad, a dark secret she'd kept for all of my life."

"Oh, shit. We aaaaall got some family drama then. You are not alone, Kylie."

"Yeah, but mine was pretty fucked up." I blew my nose. "I was a product of incest." I figured she might as well know everything.

She put her hand on her heart. "Oh, honey, I'm so sorry."

"No, it's okay. I just really gotta get it together. I don't want to be jealous of an innocent baby. It just sounds sick. I know I sound crazy. It's a baaaaby."

"No, it doesn't. We just can't let your ass babysit until you get some counseling." We both started laughing.

She was making me feel better already. "How is your mom doing? How many months and all?"

"She's two months and seems pretty happy. She can try again and do it right." I shrugged. "I guess it's good that she gets a second chance to redeem herself. But I just can't get my childhood back and do it over." I sucked my teeth.

"Well, just try your hardest to be supportive. You might be surprised and fall in love with your baby sister or brother." She tapped my leg.

I sniffed and reached for another tissue off of my nightstand. "I know I will get over it. I guess I've got a lot of healing to do."

"Chile, family is something else. We can't pick them, but we gotta deal with the cards we are dealt." She rose from the bed. "I've been through the wringer and back, and most of my family is only there when there is something in it for their greedy asses. They will extort you for a buck. That's why you won't really see me fucking with them."

"Do you have a big family?"

"Yes, two sisters and a brother. Loads of cousins, a few nieces and nephews. My mom and dad still together, but they ain't in love. More for convenience. But I just let them be. I keep to myself. When I was going through my own living hell with my ex-husband, all they cared about was the money he had. He would pay them off to find out where I was staying. That's why I don't tell nobody my business."

I was hanging off every word since she hardly ever shared details about her life.

"I ain't even tell them I'm in med school. They would be counting my future coins."

"For real? That's huge, though. But wouldn't they know you were in Dallas with them? Isn't that where you started premed?"

She had a blank stare. "Oh no, no. They're not in Dallas . . . anymore. I wasn't with them. They are in Texas just not where I am." She adjusted her head scarf to tie it tighter. "Look, Kylie, you sound like you just gotta get adjusted, but I feel your mom is trying to get it together, so just be there for her. You only got one momma. I wish I could be closer to mine, but I love her from a distance." She stretched her arms up and yawned, "Okay, girl, lemme get back to studying. I'm going back into the bat cave. You good?"

"Yes. Thank you for making me feel better."

Mackenzie smiled and closed the door slowly. Then she cracked it back open. "I made some vegan apple pie if you want some comfort food. It's right on the counter. Have you a slice or two. It tastes so good with tea."

"That sounds like a good idea. Thank you."

Maybe she was right. I might enjoy being a big sister, after all. Mom's pregnancy might bring us even closer. I only got one mom, so I will work harder on loving her and showing her how to love me.

Chapter 9

Jacques

My noon client walked in slowly. Her presence was so strong that I felt a wave of energy hit me the second she entered the room. She wore a huge white head wrap with a matching linen dress that flowed to her toes. Sheena's clenched jaw and her furrowed eyebrows didn't compliment her beautiful amber complexion or her goddess attire. Her hazel eyes scanned my office, my shoes, jeans, and T-shirt. Then she stopped in her tracks and asked suspiciously. "You're Jacques?"

I nodded and smiled, reaching out my hand to shake hers.

As she shook my hand, she said, "But Steph said you were from Africa or something."

"Well, yes, I was born in Morocco. Don't look so alarmed. We come in all shapes and colors." I shook my head with a smile.

"I don't mean to sound crazy or even rude, for that matter, but I was hoping you were like an older African witch doctor—shaman type, but you look like a . . . well, a Latino model."

We both laughed. "Why, thank you . . . I think." I shrugged my shoulders. "That's very nice of you. I'm no model, but why in the world would you need a witch doctor?"

"I need some serious magic done. I think my boyfriend has a curse on him. It's almost like he's possessed. He's not the same."

I led her to sit down. "Okay, before you tell me anything, let me get settled. I would like to meditate for a few."

I took several deep breaths and felt my body sink into the chair.

"What's his name?"

"Donavan McDowell. Do you need his middle name too?"

"No, no . . ." I closed my eyes and just saw darkness. Then to my far right, gigantic fireballs landed on the earth in flashes of blinding light. I suddenly felt my stomach drop. An intense heaviness—Fear. Darkness. I heard loud bombs dropping behind me, and I jumped in my chair. It was louder than the Fourth of July.

"What's wrong?" Sheena asked.

With my eyes still closed, I held my ears. They were ringing. "I just heard a loud noise. A bomb or explosion of some kind. I also feel extremely sad and afraid."

"Damn, Steph said you were good, but daaaamn. Donavan just came back from Syria. It was his fifth tour. He did Iraq and Afghanistan as well in the past. Infantry. Trained sniper. He was in charge of a lot of men. Some secret missions he won't even tell *me* about."

"Wow, yes, that makes sense." I closed my eyes again and took a deep breath. I put both hands on my stomach and asked my spirit guides to take the pain away in my mind. Many times, it's not an intense pain, just a little discomfort to show me how the person was feeling. Usually, when I felt a pain in my belly that indicated the person was in a deep depression or had very low self-esteem. It's the solar plexus chakra, what I like to call life's "suitcase." We stuff all of our worries there. Unfortunately, many times, it stays and grows into illnesses—even cancers.

"I have to say it's such a deep state of depression that I feel almost hollow. Like when you look into his eyes . . ."

"Oh my God. That's what is *so* scary when I look in his eyes. It's not him anymore. No one's home!" she shouted.

"Yes, he is not really all there at times. He's using a lot of drugs or alcohol to escape. Is he on some medication of some kind?"

"He's supposed to be, but he keeps saying the government is trying to kill him. That he knows too much . . . that those drugs they gave him make him too groggy, and he doesn't like them, and they are made to kill him. So, he resorts to weed and heavy liquor most of the time."

I nodded my head. "He might be under the influence right now. I feel extremely dazed and confused. That's the energy I'm picking up."

"I can see that. He stays high. Did someone put a curse on him? Why is he so out of it? He's in a fog most of the time since he got back. He's almost like a zombie. He doesn't want to do anything."

"No, noooo curse. He just has been through a lot more than he's able to share with you. He's done a lot more than you know. Now that he's home and not in fight mode, it's all hitting him. He's reliving it daily. It haunts him. He just wants to be alone at times."

In my vision, I felt as if I were him, and I could see what he saw. I was him in a small village I figured was somewhere in the Middle East. I was frantically running, going house to house, kicking open doors. I heard people screaming. I saw people drop to their knees, begging.

I could even see the uniform and boots he wore. I felt extremely powerful. He would ask no questions. Just shoot people at point-blank range in their backs or the middle of their foreheads. They looked like civilians. No uniforms. Some were women and children. I felt my heart racing, but it was a rush. It was target practice. To him, it was just like playing a video game—killing the enemy for fun.

I felt enormous guilt in my heart, and my eyes started to water. I caught a tear, quickly wiping my left eye as if something got in it. I kept them shut, not wanting to show her how much the sadness was taking over me.

I shared with her, "I think he got so desensitized out there, killing became . . ." I shuttered as I said it, "Killing was a game to him. He . . . I don't know if you are ready to hear this, Sheena."

She leaned in for details. "Please, please, tell me. I need to know. That is why I came to you."

"It seems as if he murdered a lot of innocent people. He feels the army drugged him and brainwashed him to do it. He felt under their control. He is in a state of heavy remorse now. It's almost as if he can't believe that was him, and the memories are haunting him now. Like they are someone else's memories."

"I think those military fuckers definitely did some sort of mind control on him. They turned him into a monster—I really do. If you knew Donavan, that is *not* him. That is not his heart. He loved to protect people. He wouldn't do that on purpose."

I said, "He's angry with himself. He really needs to see someone. He needs help badly."

"He won't. I asked him to see a therapist, and he refuses. He can't even be around sirens, cop cars, and loud sounds without having panic attacks. And, well, that's not just it. He cuts himself on his arms with a razor. He's been doing it almost every day. He's very angry and punches holes in doors. He has never laid a hand on our daughter or me, but I'm getting terrified. He's been back only a month, and it's only getting worse.

"I went to another psychic named Miss Lona, who said he had a family curse on him, and that if I didn't take care of it, my daughter would get it. She scared the shit out of me. I gave that bitch $350, and she said she wanted $500 more because she needed to buy these special candles to pray for him."

"Oh God, if I hear another one of these stories . . ." I looked at her in disbelief.

"No, Jacques, she got me because, like you, she was so accurate. She described him from head to toe. Knew he had tattoos on his left arm. She knew he was in the army. You are good too. You just do it a little differently. She was using some weird shells and also tarot cards."

"Okay, I'm sure she was good, but the problem is some excellent psychics are out there, but they use their gift for evil and manipulation. They reel you in with a ten-dollar tarot card or palm reading and then find a way to put fear in you so that you get addicted. The most common trap is 'the curse.'"

"Oh my goodness, she was ten dollars at first. You speaking the truth."

"Exactly. See, they wow you with their talent, gain your trust, and then you feel like they can save you. It's a con. I'm so sorry you fell for it, but I'm glad you wised up and didn't give up more. I've seen folks spend their entire life savings on these people."

"I want to beat her ass now."

"Don't bother. It always comes back to them eventually. I've even seen some arrested for fraud. They feel invincible as if they won't have to pay for their bad deeds later."

"I feel like such an idiot."

"Don't, Sheena. You are not the first to fall for it." I took a deep breath since I felt restless with Donavan's energy still inside of me. "I think it's best we get back to him."

"Yessss, please."

I held my heart. "He's lost a lot of friends over the years. He is so sad, wishing it were him that died at times. Heavy regrets. He needs help soon. He's saying to me, 'All of them are dead. They were all blown up. All of them.'"

"Oh yes, that is him," she gasped. "He really has lost almost every single close friend from his unit." She started to cry as she spoke. "I feel so alienated, so helpless. We were supposed to get married this year. But now, I don't know. I don't want to be afraid. I think you're my last hope."

"I'm not. I can give you insight, but he definitely will need to get some help. It's just hard now. He's getting adjusted to being home. He will be somewhat better in a couple of weeks."

I passed Sheena a tissue, and she wiped her tears. We used the remaining time of her session to discuss her health, her daughter, and I gave her some meditations and tips to keep her blood pressure down. Her health was in jeopardy because she was worried about her man.

I really hoped Donavan got the help he needed because sometimes, it just goes downhill if they stay in denial. I felt confident that he would be open to help, just not right now.

***

After Sheena left, I walked down the hall to Like a Fly on the Wall, and Vince had the TV on a sports show on full blast. The door cracked, and his chair squeaked as he swirled around to see who it was.

"Hey, hey. If it isn't my favorite Magic Man." He reached for the remote to turn down the loud football commentary.

"Hey, Vince."

"Kylie should be here in a minute, but let me catch you up to speed on the progress we made on the last case you helped us with." He pulled up a document on his computer. "The Raymond case is closed. You were on the money when you told us to look into the husband's real estate purchases. Turns out this guy had not just one, but two condos he purchased under his business's names. He was so slick to have two girlfriends living in them. The wife was livid but very happy we were able to trace it back to him. He apparently even used some of *her* money to purchase the properties."

"Wow, that is great news. I knew there were layers to his story. He has some assets hidden as well, like just money. Did you look into that?"

"Yes, he had some accounts moved to the Virgin Islands. She is going to recoup all of that in the divorce, hopefully. The wife had more than enough proof of his infidelities. Antonio staked out the apartments and caught him with his little college-aged girlfriend coming out of one."

"You guys are on it. Now, what about this new case?"

The door opened, and Kylie said, "What? You guys meeting without me?" She was holding Chinese food, and it smelled soooo good. I knew it was fish or meat, and I couldn't eat it.

Vince chimed in. "Relax, we knew you were close. I was just catching him up on the Raymond case, telling Jacques how valuable he is to us."

"Ah, that's sweet. So, you do have a heart deep down in there." Kylie giggled as she pointed at Vince's chest. "Lemme go put this in the kitchen, and I'll jump in."

"Smells good. What's in the bag?" I said.

"Shrimp and broccoli. Sorry, Mr. Vegan."

"Whatever." I waved her off.

"Jacques, we got some granola bars in the kitchen cabinet. You vegan guys can eat that, right?" Vince laughed.

"I'm good, Vince. I have my lunch in my office." I shook my head and smiled.

"Okay, I'm ready." Kylie powered up her MacBook.

"This new case involves worker's comp insurance fraud for Gordon and Gordon Construction. Seems like the employer was tipped off that this guy, Mao Dae Kim, was a mastermind of scams. He was a supervisor, and one of his own people gave him up." Vince placed a folder with a headshot and copies of Mao's claim in front of me.

The moment I saw Mao's face, my throat tightened up. He was a pretty nice-looking Asian man. Looked very professional in his headshot. However, from just a glance, I got a feeling of a cunning man. Very intelligent, but also greedy. I cleared my throat. "I already get that he is definitely hiding more than we know." I felt a heavy pressure on my shoulders, back, and throat. "He has a lot of secrets, I feel."

Kylie read an email from her computer. "We need some insight to find out what the hell he is hiding before we waste more time on surveillance. Seems like he is building a case to sue. Antonio's schedule is already slammed, and we don't have enough manpower to follow this guy every day. The tip the employer got was that he faked a back injury, and now he is suing the company on top of that. We have been trying to catch him in the act, but no luck as yet."

Vince said, "Today, we started monitoring his cell phone activity to see where he was going."

"Oh, you do that too?" I raised my eyebrows.

"Of course. I have my ways." Vince rocked back and forth in his chair. "We need you to read this guy to see if he's doing anything shady."

"Can I take this file?"

Vince took a sip of his coffee. "Sure, go ahead, Jacques. You need it to do your hocus-pocus?"

"Vince, come on. Don't make fun of the man's gift."

"It's okay, Kylie. I'm used to Vince's humor." I shook my head at him and playfully rolled my eyes.

"You got something already from looking at his picture? The secrets?"

Kylie said, "Vince, I told you, he can feel your energy instantly. He doesn't even really need a photo, either."

"Yes, but I can get way more in meditation. Give me a day to pull up something, and I'll send you my findings."

"Man, I gotta say, when Kylie mentioned this idea of having a psychic on the team, I thought it was a little kooky. Back in my day in Brooklyn, the fellas at my precincts would call this woo-woo bullshit."

"Vince," Kylie scolded.

"Hear me out." He raised his hands. "I did the numbers from last month, and our business has increased by over 30 percent in one freakin' month. I was gonna wait until Antonio was here to tell you all, but I couldn't wait."

"Oh, that's so good, Jacques." Kylie shook my shoulder and patted me on the back.

"Yeah, and what's good is Antonio appreciates it. With all your mind-reading, there is less surveillance needed and less money I gotta shell out for gas." We all laughed.

"Glad it's working out for all of us. I really enjoy it."

"Cool, so are we done, fellas? I'm starviiiing."

"Yeah, go eat, Kylie." Vince shooed her off to the kitchen.

"All right, guys. I'm going to head out. Kylie, email the info you have, OK?"

"Sure."

"Enjoy your lunch. I'm going to eat mine right now."

Vince rocked in his chair, and it squeaked so loud. "What is it? A grass sandwich with Mayo?"

"Yeah, Vince, but no Mayo. That's not vegan. But actually, it's a South Western pasta salad with tofu."

"Sounds delicious." He stuck his finger down his throat to imitate vomiting, then reached for the remote.

"Later, guys."

The TV went back to full blast.

"Aye, Vince. Turn it down, please. I can't think straight. You're making me deaf. You should get your ears checked."

I nodded in agreement as I gently closed the door.

Jacques

Today was a light day with only two clients before lunch, but I planned it like that on purpose since I had to get my baby brother from the airport. Only five days ago, he called me with a last-minute request, and being the kind, pushover big brother I am, I said yes.

***

"Yo, Jay."

"Hey, Hicham." I smiled at the sound of my brother's voice. "Where the hell you been? Haven't heard from you in over a week."

"Grinding, man. I've been busy with work, but I'm taking a break and gonna work on a few freelance projects this month, but, hey—they're in Miami."

"Oh, really, now?" I knew what was coming next.

"So, since you living the single life now, can I crash with you for a couple of weeks? Maybe even just ten days?"

"Weeks, huh? When are you arriving?"

"Friday good? I am buying a one-way."

"Wow, talk about a short notice."

"I need a change in scenery anyhow."

"Sure, you can stay. But let me be very clear—"

"Oh booooy, here he go."

"I don't want a bunch of women parading through my house. You can get a hotel room for that."

"Oh, come on. I can't have company? Like I'm a little kid?"

"Hicham, I know you. I don't want your riffraff chicks in my house. You bring home puppies off the street. I don't like people knowing where I live."

"I'll just go to their house then. You just hating 'cause you ain't getting none. You need to pull that stick outta your ass."

"Whatever."

"I could get us some fine-ass models."

"No, thanks. Just text me the time to pick you up, and I'll come get you."

"Bet."

Friday came so quickly. I made it to the Miami International Airport just in time. While I was waiting for Hicham's plane to land, I got an Instagram alert. Not one, not two, but *three* likes from Vicky. My stomach flipped. As silly as it sounded, I felt a glimmer of hope. I was on her mind.

My clients obsess over social media, and, unfortunately, I think it's rubbing off on me. Whose photo their husband is liking? What emojis are being used on their wives' sexy pictures, and which guy posted it. They turn one simple smiling face or hearts into massive affairs, when most of the time, it's purely someone just liking the darn photo. I hope that I can set up another "friendship date" again soon with Vicky to see where her head was at now. I would not pressure her, but I will definitely try again.

I saw a bus drive by with an ad promoting the latest medium show on HBO. I thought about how Vicky always said I would be good on TV and encouraged me to connect with the few clients I had in L.A. who were producers in order to secure a talk-show gig. She would always cheer me on and give me feedback on ideas. I missed that. I even missed her hair clogging up the bathroom tub. It's crazy how you end up missing the things that used to annoy you when a loved one vanishes. The saddest thing is I had so many good things happening in my life right now and no one to share it with. I had my friends Kylie and Melissa, my brother, and a few other friends. However, that wasn't as satisfying as coming home to the person that would share in your success.

Hicham's plane finally arrived, and who I saw come out of the airport surprised me. I saw his lanky frame walking toward my car with a slight bop and slow, long-legged strides, like some dude that did hard time or was in a gang from a rough part of town. But no, baby bro was really a squeaky-clean Catholic school kid from SOHO who dreamed of being Tupac someday. He was a bit temperamental, however, so, thankfully, he never became a rapper. He would have definitely been in jail by now. They feel invincible as if they won't have to pay for their bad deeds later. Lucky for him, he ended up being an amazing photographer and popular relationship columnist instead.

He came outside just in time before the traffic cop came back for me on his intimidating scooter. He told me to drive around twice already, and I did not care to do it again. I pointed to Hicham to let the airport cop know he was who I was waiting for. As he got closer, he resembled the Grim Reaper in a dark hoodie. This was *not* my little brother. My throat got tight and dry, my heart sank, and my stomach churned. Too much going on. I was picking up a lot of bad energy around him. His eyes were glassy, and he had a scraggly goatee.

I jumped out of the car to help him with his bags. He had a lot of camera equipment. He gave me a pound, and then we hugged. I missed him. I put my hands on his shoulder to get a good look at him.

"Hicham, what's going on, man? You not getting any sleep?"

"Negative. None at all. I haven't been sleeping well in months, man, you know, since Mom."

"Yeah, I know."

"Look, I know I look like shit, so don't start."

A whistle shrieked, almost blowing out our eardrums. The cop was on his scooter, waving for us to hurry and stop the chatter.

"A'ight, man, we getting out of your way. Be easy." Hicham screamed at the cop a little too aggressive if you ask me. He turned to me, "Look at this Robocop motherfucker on his little scooter. He ain't get accepted into the marines, and now he wanna boss people around." He put his bags in the trunk more slowly than needed just to be a jerk.

"Hicham, just get in the car."

We were in back-to-back traffic. He and his last-minute flight. I should have told him not to arrive during Miami rush-hour.

"So, Hicham, what's new and exciting in your world?"

"Man, not much. I'm just happy to be out of the city. I needed a change, so I booked a few projects. They've been begging me to come for the longest."

I looked in his face, and I still couldn't believe how worn he looked. He was only three years younger than I was, and he looked 40. His party-animal lifestyle was catching up to him, for sure. Losing our mom weighed extra heavy on him since he was the cause of her accident. He never got officially blamed, but the guilt has plagued him, and he hasn't been quite the same since. He hides his pain with humor, and I guess it works since he always knows how to make people laugh. It helps him take his mind off of his own problems.

"So, what's up witchuuu, thoooough? You looking all fresh and clean. Looking lean and shit. Swole. You get any new pussy yet?"

"Well . . . now that you mention it." I smiled, thinking about Dee's sexy body doing that dance for me.

"Naaaah, say, word. You finally broke your chastity belt?" He slapped the dashboard, laughing at his own jokes.

"Shut up." I mushed him in the head with one hand, keeping the other hand on the steering wheel. Finally, the traffic was letting up, so I was able to speed up.

"Come on. You was holding out waiting on Vicky to come back after she left your ass."

"Hicham, why do you have to be so cold? That shit is not funny. Not funny."

"Okay, okaaaay. My bad. So, who is it?"

"No one you know. She's an old friend from NYC who was in town."

"Oh shit. Well, I'm glad. I was beginning to worry about you. You know you can't disappoint these Miami bitches. Don't let them pretty-boy looks go to waste. There is soooo much ass to get down here, it's crazy."

"Whatever. We are also number one with HIV in the nation, let's not forget that, dear horny little brother."

"Truuuue, truuuue." He nodded his head in agreement. "You seem to have another talent other than seeing the future."

I tilted my head, confused.

"'Cause, you always gotta fuck shit up." He rolled his eyes.

We got to my condo, and he made himself at home in my guest bedroom. After he unpacked a bit, he joined me in the living room.

"Well, I'm gonna be doing a few shoots in Wynwood this weekend for a new bikini line. If you wanna roll with me . . . We can have some fun."

"I'll think about it, but you know we don't have the same idea of fun, and we definitely don't enjoy the same type of women." I already knew I wasn't going. The women he hung out with were not my type—all body and no brains. Most couldn't even carry on a sensible conversation without asking you about reality TV, sex, or talk about their aspirations to be a video vixen. I think I'd keep my options open, but my heart wasn't ready for the drama.

"Whatever. Type of women?" He snorted, "Women are women. They all got the same thing, and they all want the same thing."

"Oh, and what would that be, wise old sage?"

"Good dick and good food. They love food but go heavy on the good dick. You stroke them right, and they'll do whatever you want."

"Oh, did you write an article about that?"

"As a matter of fact, I did. May edition—'What a Woman Wants—That Vitamin D.'"

I slapped my forehead. "Really?"

"So, hold up—you not reading my shit no more? You were my biggest fan at one point."

"Of course, you know I always support what you do. I'm just a little bit behind in reading. Been busy, but that Vitamin D . . . I'll make a mental note." I sarcastically tapped my temple.

"Oh, you got jokes? Why you so busy, anyway? You don't do shit but read them pathetic people's minds, hear them talk about all they stupid problems, and then you go home and play with your dick."

I held in a laugh but punched him hard in his arm.

We both started cracking up. He should have been a damn comedian. He loved to run his mouth. "Damn, bro, you been lifting? You punching like a real brolic motherfucker now. What happened to the love taps you used to give me?" He was rubbing his bicep in pain.

I did punch him a bit harder than expected. I couldn't help it. That mouth makes you want to hurt him. That will shut him up for at least a half hour.

"You need to eat and do some push-ups for that scrawny frame of yours. I don't know what kinda strokes you're delivering to all of your so-called women if you can barely do a push-up."

I chuckled and watched him in my fridge like a scavenger looking for food.

"See, that's where you're wrong. That's the benefit of being slim. My body is not so big, soooo all the blood rushes to where it needs to go." He paused and shouted, "My diiiick."

"Yeah, whatever." I waved him off. "You're a fool, you know that?"

"Yo, what's up with all this rabbit food? What is you doing—a fast?"

"Sorry, I'm vegetarian now . . . well, semi. I do some fish. You came at short notice, but we can get groceries tomorrow. You want to go out for dinner now? It's on me."

"Word? Bet."

Chapter 10

Kylie

I was at the office early on Friday, checking on all of my social media accounts before the fellas came in. It was my guilty pleasure that made me laugh at some of the pickup lines from these guys. So many men, but the options were few. Chauncey, I really enjoyed, but he was so far away, and he acted so scared of sex that it's a bit weird. I'm not sure if I intimidated him or what. He was hot and heavy on our first date, but things have slowed down tremendously, and him living four hours north in Orlando doesn't help. The red flag was when I got hate mail in my FB inbox from his crazy ex-girl a couple of months ago. Drama and I ain't friends, so I'm on the fence about his ass. He calls and texts me consistently, and he claims she was crazy and not in the picture, but we'll see.

I also met BIGHEART83, aka Mario—no last name given yet—a cute Italian dude originally from the Bronx. He kinda looked like a younger George Clooney, or at least his cousin. He said he was a "complete chocoholic" and very down with Jamaican culture. His ex-wife was Jamaican. I wasn't trying to be his first Black girl like I was an experiment, so that was cool to know. Shit, he knew more than me about the food and culture of the Caribbean. I loved talking to him on the phone. He made me laugh so much. Only problem is that he's in Las Vegas running an import/export business. Sucks for me. He keeps promising to fly to Miami. We'll see.

Those are the good options . . . Then you have the corny guys who send you generic copy-and-paste emails that start off with . . .

"You're the one for me"

"Hey, beautiful . . ."

"Oh, I love me a natural sista"

Or they have the infamous bathroom selfie holding their shirt up to show you their abs in a filthy bathroom.

My ultimate favorites are what I like to call *pillow shots* . . . Those are photos they take from their pillow with the camera facing down on them so that it feels like you are on top of them. Very, very sexy.

Jacques is always teasing me about the guys I met online. He said that he wished most of his female clients had as many options as I did. But my options were never within *booty call limits*. The guys I met that were the most compatible were more than 400 miles away.

Breeze was coming to visit soon, so that was something to look forward to. Madame Butterfly will stop fluttering and relax for a bit. When I see him, he would take away all of my anxiety—the perfect cure and stress reliever.

I logged out of my username on Facebook and logged into my spyware site to check on Rubia's online communication. We had a meeting last week, and Antonio said that the client wanted more solid information that he could show her and the courts to prove she was cheating. He even paid extra for Antonio to use his spyware glasses to take photos. Some real James Bond shit.

Facebook

Rubia's account

Rubia: Meet me tonight. Charlie's Den for Lovers. I'm bringing two friends.

Sergio: My love, you bring your friends with you. I can watch. I just want you after. I've been craving that pussy all week. I wanna fuck you hard and deep. Are you ready for me?

Rubia: I know, baby, I want you too. I miss you. We have so much fun together. I'm all yours tonight. My husband is out of town, so we can stay out all night if we want. I'm going to do so many wonderful things to you that you will forget all of your troubles. Be there at 9.

Sergio: You already have. I can't stop thinking about you. I will be there waiting. I look forward to meeting your friends.

Oh shit. It's on. I took a screen shot of the convo. It didn't get much better than this as far as proof goes. I didn't think Antonio could use the screen shot in court since we essentially hacked into her account, but he could lie and say she left it open. Then Antonio walked in with a big cup of black coffee for himself from the coffee shop downstairs. He brought me a green tea like he always did.

"Why, thank you, sir. Good morning." I took a sip.

"Morning, Kylie. Boy, you are in a good mood. What's up with you?"

I handed him a printout of the screen shot. "*Pow!*"

"Oh, wow, this is big. This is huge. And I got my glasses? It's payday, for sure."

"Yep, we gonna get all the info tonight."

He wrinkled his nose. "We? Hold up . . . You want to come? You don't have to."

"Are you kidding? I wanna see this, especially if you're taking photos."

"Cool, well, let's get that work in. Remember, this is off the books. It's my account, not Vince's, so don't say nothing."

"I got you."

***

Vince ended up calling in sick, so the day was hectic. We had a lot of new clients coming in from the online ads I placed, so I was beyond busy. Antonio was out on a surveillance job for an insurance fraud case. So, I was alone for most of the day. I only had green tea and a papaya smoothie all day. Then I had to rush home to be there early for Antonio to pick me up to go to Charlie's Den for the Rubia case.

I got home so late, at about 8:00 p.m., so I hardly had time to take a shower and get cute. My stomach growled as I remembered I was supposed to stop at the supermarket on the way home. What I had in the freezer was going to take too long to cook. I put some water on the stove to make some mint tea, and I stole a brownie from the Tupperware on the counter.

I wrote on a Post-it Note even though Mackenzie probably wouldn't care. I didn't want to overstep and take advantage of her generosity.

Post-it:
My bad, don't kill me. I took one. Starving and late for a job tonight. I can buy you more.

I slipped into an orange miniskirt and cream, low-cut camisole. I had my hair up in a French roll and big gold bangles and earrings to match. I added a spritz of perfume since Antonio was probably going to be up on me, "acting." I think part of me really loved flirting with him even though it was work. I might as well play my part too.

My phone vibrated from a text. Antonio was outside. I got two sips of tea and inhaled the brownie before leaving. "Wow, that shit was delicious," I said to the Tupperware bowl I got it from, thinking about snatching another one. But I decided not to be greedy and headed out.

"Legs, legs, legs for days." He whistled and said, "You should wear dresses and skirts more." He tilted his new Clark Kent glasses to take a photo.

"Stop it."

"Nah, I had to take a photo of that."

"You look like a real nerd, but it fits you."

"They look official, right? No one would ever know I had a camera in here. They don't allow cameras in there at all. I might make some money blackmailing everyone up in there." He laughed. "You know I've seen some high-profile people in there. Police, senators, professors, a lot of people. But it's like a secret society, so no one is telling."

I smiled to myself since he told me before he's only been there twice for the job. Sounded like a regular to me.

We entered Charlie's Den for Lovers, and when we got to the club area, we stood by the glass room again with all of the beds.

Antonio was dancing behind me and whispered, "There she goes, right on time." He pointed to his watch that said 9:00 p.m. Rubia entered the club walking slowly and looking around for her friends.

She passed by and touched Antonio's shoulder and floated by, saying, "Hey, Will."

"What up, Rubia? This is Nia."

I smiled and nodded as Antonio caressed my stomach and hips. I was tingling out of control. I couldn't believe I was getting paid to do this. I almost forgot this was work. I felt moist. Antonio's masculinity was overwhelming.

"Damn, girl, your acting is pretty good today. You loosened waaaay up." I was actually grinding on him to "Back that Ass Up," by Juvenile.

"Did you get that photo of her just now or too dark?"

"Did you get that photo of her just now or too dark?"

"Of course. And I can adjust the lighting when I edit. These glasses are official."

Apparently, when you tilt or press the button on the side, it triggers a silent snapshot.

"You know we gotta catch her in the act. In there." He pointed to the glass room of lust. "You can stay over here if you want, Ky. Beyond this point, you gotta be naked. But you can wear a towel."

I *wanted* to see him naked. I *wanted* to watch. The entire environment was turning me on. The music got louder, and I started dancing.

"Oh shit, this is my song."

"Oh yeah? I didn't know you were a Rihanna fan. You always playing white-boy music or old school."

"Whatever, Antonio."

He looked at me sternly, shaking his head in disapproval.

"I mean, Will. Will." I giggled.

"*Wild, wild, wild thoughts. When I'm with you, all I get is wild thoughts.*" He sang along with me. I had my hands in the air feeling the music. I had never before heard the song in a club over loudspeakers. "This is giving me liiiife," I yelled as I did a little Chicago Stepping. I felt so happy.

He grabbed me close. "Yo, was you drinking before I got you? You turning up tonight. What's in that cup?" He took it and smelled it.

"Nothing. I just feel good," I laughed loudly.

"I don't know, but I like *this* Kylie a lot." He moved closer behind me and held me as we danced. He kissed me on my neck. It didn't seem like he was acting since no one could see us where we were.

"Look, there go our boy with the ponytail. That's Sergio."

"Wow, he's built, but damn—his arms," I giggled. "Reminds me of Popeye."

"He probably on them steroids. Look at this fool with his long ponytail."

Rubia was on a bed with two of her friends, and he started to crawl on the bed with them. Her girlfriends were good-looking people, not supermodels, but they looked like soccer moms that did yoga and jogged. This was their "other" hobby.

Rubia took her playmate Sergio's ponytail and yanked it hard. It looked like they were arguing, but it was just role-playing. "They like it rough," Antonio mumbled as he pointed with his chin.

Sergio picked up her small frame in the air and put her to his face as if she were sitting in a chair. "Wow. He's strong." I looked at Antonio.

Sergio burrowed his face in between her legs, and from the looks of it, he was talented. She was thrashing about, clearly a woman in ecstasy. I didn't realize it, but I was grabbing Antonio's hands tightly.

"I gotta go in there and get the money shot," Antonio whispered while tapping his Clark Kent glasses. My ear was warm from his breath. I didn't know what was going on, but he aroused me.

Then things got fuzzy. There were the smells in the locker room. A combination of pheromones and latex that gave off an animalistic vibe. An anything-goes atmosphere. I could feel a towel around my waist. My breasts were bare. I felt free, not afraid. Anthony sat on a bed next to me, and I knew this was wrong, but I couldn't stop myself. I was floating . . . feeling so good and euphoric. He hugged me from behind and held my breasts until the towel fell off. I felt his hardness on my back. I was sweating and out of breath. My hair was wet. I was missing time. I didn't know how long we were there.

"What's going on? When did we get-get naked?" The room was spinning. Colors were everywhere like I was inside of a Kaleidoscope. I actually saw spots.

"Kylie, why you tripping? You sure you ain't drink nothing? Did you put your drink down earlier?" He smiled big. "Come on, let me eat that pussy again. You taste so gooood, baby."

Again? When did he ever . . . what? Eat. My. Pussy? This can't be happening. He put the glasses on his head and lay down. I felt so heavy, like lead. My entire body was tingling, and I couldn't wipe the smile off of my face. I suddenly felt soft hands touching on my thighs, my breasts, my stomach. Someone was stroking my hair. I looked down and saw Antonio in between my legs sucking on my thighs. It felt soooo good. He started to taste me, and his talented tongue knew what to do.

I felt waves go throughout my body—multiple orgasms. The music got louder, and I heard sighs and screams. They weren't just mine. There were people behind me, in front of me, on the sides of me. Someone started kissing me. My eyes were closed. My body began to shiver. I was overstimulated, and I came again. Sweat cascaded down my back. The music came to a sudden stop, and the room was dark. My heart was beating so hard. I felt another wave penetrate my body. My coochie was tingling. I was covered in sweat.

I must have been dreaming. That was a nasty-ass dream. Shit, I must have fallen asleep watching a porno or something. I felt warmth next to me and then heard a light snore. I turned to my left and realized I wasn't alone—and I wasn't home. His broad chocolate back was facing me. He was breathing deeply. I panicked, my heart racing, wondering—

What

Did

I

Do?

Chapter 11

Kylie

My first instinct was to get up and run, but I didn't know where to. The warmth of the bed and his snoring told me we had been sleeping for a while. My heart sped up as my eyes darted around the dark room, trying to figure out how we even got here. I shook his shoulder. "Antonio! Antonio! Where are we?"

He turned around slowly, saying in a groggy voice, "Kylie, yo. Can you chill out? It's early, baby. Gimme a few. We at my crib. Chiiiill."

I sat up. "What? Your crib? But how? I don't . . . I don't remember coming here." I felt nausea rising. My heart pounded in my chest as I searched for memories. I couldn't place how I was missing time.

He rolled over on his back and leaned toward me. "Well, I don't know what you was on last night, baby, but daaaamn, you was a freeeeak. I had to get you outta Charlie's Den. Everyone wanted a piece of that ass."

I sat up in shock. "Charlie's? We went there?"

He nodded with eyebrows raised.

I just saw all of those hands touching me. "So, that wasn't a dream? Did we . . .?"

"We fooled around." He sat up. "You mean you reaaaally don't remember?" His feelings looked hurt.

"Yo, Antonio, I'm bugging out right now. I swear now I kinda remember being at Charlie's. We went to find

Rubia and take photos, right? I remember dancing to Rihanna, but then the rest I felt was a dream. I thought maybe it was *all* a dream." I held my heart, preparing myself. "So, when you say 'fooled around,' what do you mean?"

He moved the sheet back to show me his very trim and muscular naked body. He was semihard, and it looked rather nice, but I was so embarrassed. "Antonio, OMG. What the fuck." I covered my eyes.

He sat up. "Kylie, you were deep throating me like a pro last night. Now you wanna be bashful?"

I looked down at my body, and I was still in the same clothes. I got up to look in his dresser mirror. My makeup was gone, and my hair was a mess. I felt under my skirt. My panties were still on.

"I dressed myself?"

"Yes, after fighting me for making you leave the glass room. I thought maybe you were a little tipsy, but—"

My hands were shaking, and I sat back down next to him. "I think someone drugged me. Someone fucking drugged me, Antonio. They had to have. I remember my head feeling weird. I remember floating and feeling high. Do they spike drinks there with ecstasy or something? Is that even a thing? Antonio, why didn't you take me home sooner? I gotta take a shower. This is so gross. Did anyone else do anything?"

"Slow down. Noooo, no one fucked you. You was just getting felt up . . . a lot." He smiled a guilty smile. "Ky, whatever it was you took, you best not take it again around me 'cause the next time, I won't be a gentleman. Your head game is *madness*." He chuckled and shook his head wildly. "I was finna put a hurting on you last night. Boy, you don't know." He put his finger on my lips.

I wished I could remember. "So, I sucked your—"

"Yes, and, well . . . and I ate you—"

"Stop! Stop!" I ran to the bathroom to wash my face. I screamed, "This is too much."

"Kylie, I think you should know . . . there was a guy there that knew you too. He looked familiar, but I couldn't remember where I saw him before. Maybe in the office building or something? When everything was going down, he was with some girls watching. I think if I didn't get you out, they were gonna make a move to join our bed."

"What did he look like? Oh God. Someone that kneeeew me? This is so crazy."

"Man, I wasn't all up in his face. Men don't do that shit, especially there. But he said your name, and I just ignored him. He was a white dude. Dark hair, tall . . . but that's all I could tell you. I was kinda distracted by you. You kept me busy, baby." He rubbed my thigh.

"Okaaaay, enough, Antonio, this is *not* funny. You know I could have been raped, gangbanged? I could have a disease. That place is filthy."

"First of all, they don't let shit like that go down, and I was there with you. Ain't nobody fucking touching you on my watch."

"Well, you said there were hands on me and people kissing me."

"Yeah, but you were enjoying it, so I let them. Fucking you is another story." He paused. "I thought we really had something going and was looking to take it further when we got to my house. I didn't want to share you anymore. But when we got here, you conked out on the bed. I don't take advantage of a corpse."

The sun started to rise outside.

"Where's my phone, my purse? Do you . . .?"

"You left your phone in my car. It's charging over there next to your purse." He pointed to the nightstand next to my side of the bed.

I didn't want Mackenzie to worry, so I turned on my phone and immediately five texts came in . . . all from Mackenzie.

11:50 p.m. Mackenzie: Kylie, do not eat that brownie, please.

12:35 a.m. Mackenzie: Kylie, call me back immediately.

2:00 a.m. Mackenzie: Call me, please. That was for a client who has PTSD. Very potent. Do not eat.

4:42 a.m. Mackenzie: Where are you? Please call me. It's urgent. Please tell me you didn't eat that whole thing.

"Oh shit. It was the brownie," I said to Antonio.

"What?"

Mackenzie picked up on the first ring, and I put my finger up to Antonio to let him know I was on a call.

"Oh God, Kylie, I've been fucking worried sick." She sounded like an alarmed mother. "What happened to you? I didn't want to txt it, but that was an edible brownie."

"Edible, as in has weed?"

"Yes, not just any kind, though. It has a special strain for people who have PTSD or chronic pain. How much of it did you eat? Where are you?"

"I'm safe. Just shaken up a bit. Shit. I just knew someone drugged me. I'm glad it was you." We laughed. "I'm at Antonio's. I ate the whole thing last night, girl."

"Whaaaat! That is *Triple Grade-A Kush*. Chile, you must have been high as a kite."

"I don't remember things. Like I blacked out. I was floating, seeing colors, and was so damn horny. Shit, serves me right for touching the shaman's food," I chuckled.

"Oh, hush. You gave me the scare of my life, girl."

"I'll be home soon. I'm somewhat relieved it wasn't some crazy pill put in my drink."

She sighed. "Just so happy you are okay. I definitely did not want you driving. You could think you seeing spaceships and Big Bird in the road and try to dodge them and end up in a tree."

"Oh no. Thank God, I wasn't driving."

"Chile, you know the prescription for my clients is only one-fourth of what you ate?"

"Damn, and I inhaled that whole big-ass brownie in five minutes."

"You are blessed; you don't even know. I wouldn't be able to live with myself if something happened to my little buttercup."

"Well, I'm okay, but now I know about *yet another talent*. What *don't* you do?"

"Well, it's one of my hustles to pay for med school."

"I wanna be like you when I grow up. Well, I'll be home soon."

Antonio slid on his jeans, and I got a good view of his very nice ass. He saw me checking him out and smiled, then went into the bathroom and started brushing his teeth.

I yelled to him, "So, it was a brownie—edibles for sick clients. My roommate is like a damn witch doctor. She's a healer." I stood behind him while he brushed his teeth bare-chested.

He washed his mouth and wiped it with a towel. "Shit, I'm gonna have to buy a batch more from her. That shit was powerful." He raised his eyebrows with a smile.

I rolled my eyes. "Well, I took too much. You're only supposed to eat one-fourth. I ate the whole thing."

"Ky, you are the truth." He pumped his fist in the air.

"Come on, stop it. I feel so weird because I really don't remember much."

"You want me to remind you?" He hugged me. "I'm just messing with you. If you and me ever cross that line again, you just gonna have to quit your job, 'cause I'm fucking the shit out of you, and I want you 100 percent alert. You have a beautiful body, though. I mean, beautiful, and your pussy is so—"

I slapped his chest. "I can't take this. I'm so humiliated."

"Don't be, don't be. Not to mention, I got mad photos for our client. I'm about to up the price per photo on his ass."

"Wow, that's good. I'm tired."

He handed me a paper cup. "You cute and all, but you got morning breath like the rest of us." I looked in the mirror and got a better look at myself. I had one crusted eye, and my French roll was totally gone and now a flattened Gumby-shaped 'fro.

"Hand me a washcloth, please, and mouthwash. And stop laughing at meeee," I whined.

"You make it easy to make fun of you, Ky. You are a sweetheart, though, you know that? You try to be all tough—that Brooklyn talk, but you really have a big heart. You care about people. I see how hard you work."

"Ah, Antonioooo." I wiped my face with the washcloth.

"Nah, for real. You're really growing on me. So, I thought maybe this was just opening the door to a new side of our friendship. No pressure, but, damn, I can't lie. I want some more of that, and I'm feeling a way that you don't remember anything."

"I-I don't know what to say. I really like you, Antonio, but I'm trying to take this in."

Wow, look at him expressing his feelings. I was torn because a part of me was flattered and curious about what would go down now that I had my senses about me. But mostly, I was still disgusted by what I did last night. And thankful. I believed Antonio when he said he didn't take advantage of me. I know how I felt after I've been fucked, and I didn't feel anything. The fact that he didn't take it all the way says a lot about his character.

"Well, maybe we can talk more about this." I didn't want to start something so close to home. You know that old saying, don't eat where you shit?

Also, he must be a serious freak. He might be too much for me to handle. Could I even trust him?

"Antonio, I think I should go. Can you take me home now?"

"I will. I got you. Let me jump in the shower real quick. We can pick up breakfast on the way, if you hungry. Or I can make you some eggs?" He shrugged his shoulders as if he were trying to give it one last shot.

I sat on the bed, thumbing through my text messages.

"No, no, it's okay." Wow, I must have really been spectacular last night. When a dude wants to make you breakfast, *that's* special. "I just wanna go home and shower myself. Like ten times. I'm still shaken up."

He shook his head and closed the door, turning on the shower. "I didn't mean it like that," I mumbled. Hope I didn't hurt his feelings.

Fuck . . . Antonio. Breeze. Chauncey. I'm really in trouble. Jacques always teased me, but maybe he was right. Too many men, too little time . . .

Chapter 12

Kylie

The birds were chirping loudly to welcome me home. The sun was shining brightly, and it was already a very warm 79 degrees. I put my key in the front door, but before I could turn the handle, it was yanked open. Mackenzie shocked me, donning a jet-black bob wig I never saw before. She had on her apron that said, "*Kiss Me, I'm Vegan.*" And the aroma of cake floated out the door.

I held my heart and laughed. "Girl, you almost had me pull out my kickboxing moves. You and your disguises—like you're an undercover spy."

"Chile, please, I just like to switch it up. I get bored easily." She ushered me inside with her arm on my shoulder.

"And, again, I'm so, so sorry, girl. I should have told you about my side gig. I just didn't want to give you the wrong idea."

I nodded. "It's all good. You baking this early?"

"Yes, I have work today, and I have clients who want their pies tonight." She cocked her head to the side. "You look terrible. Let me see your pupils." She put her warm hand under my chin and grabbed my face.

"Why, thanks, Doc." I overexaggerated an eye bulge and tilted my head back for her to exam me.

"Jesus, they so glassy."

"Don't worry. All I had was a soda and a spiked brownie," I smirked. "It was a very, very long night. I just want to sleep. I don't remember much, but it's coming back to me in little visions. I know one thing. I will never *evaaa* eat your food again without asking."

"So, girl, for real? You ate the *whole* thang. Like the whole block? That shit is my top seller. You had enough for four people."

"Potent enough to have me sucking my coworker's dick." I sat down by the bar in the kitchen.

"What? Shut up," she laughed. "Is he fine, though?"

"Yeah, he's hot," I smiled. "So, hold up. How do you even know how to make these kinds of brownies? Is there a class or something? A YouTube video?"

Mackenzie took off her apron and started putting dishes in the dishwasher. "Well, when I was in London, one of my flat mates used to have terrible seizures. She was a bit of a hippy and smoked a lot of weed. I mean, morning, noon, and night."

"London? Wow, when did you live there?"

"Oh, I've lived soooo many places . . . not long." She cleared her throat and started opening the oven and checking on the food. "But, listen, after I learned about the recipe, I joined a few pro-medical marijuana groups, and we started swapping recipes. I found out how to get my own medical marijuana card for anxiety, so if I ever have any on me, I can't get arrested. I still have to buy off the street when I have a lot of orders, but I have a great connect. I did it for a few folks I knew who had glaucoma in a nursing home I volunteered for in Pembroke Pines."

I said in a slow yawn, "Woooow, this so cool. They getting lit in the nursing homes?"

"No, baby, they getting healed. Soon, I learned about the different strands of weed so I could, you know, prescribe it. I had a nice side hustle. I had to slow down on the nursing homes 'cause some of them elders talk too damn much, and I don't have a license to sell it. They got that Alzheimer's and shit. They might not follow instructions and end up in an orgy like your hot-in-the-pants ass did." Mackenzie smiled hard, waiting for my reaction.

"Stop it," I slapped the counter. "Stop."

"I'm serious. Them old people are freaks. I ain't lying. Girl, I'm so relieved you are okay. That was hurting my heart." She held her chest dramatically.

"That blackout shit is scary, so never again. I think I'm staying clear of 'edibles.'"

"You don't have to stay clear, just know the recommended dosage and you be good."

"Yeah, okaaaay." I shook my head. "I'm gonna take my high ass to the shower and bed."

"All right, girl. Good night . . . even though it's only 8:00 a.m. now."

After a full day of sleeping, I was back to myself again. The next morning, the sultry grooves of Conya Doss were blasting in the office from my laptop. I was tapping my foot and singing along. I loved when Vince was not here. He didn't like music. He'd rather have the TV on, and it was soooo annoying. We fought about it every now and then since I would tell him how having the toxic news brings the energy down in the office. Anything that would affect work getting done would make him cower and let me listen to music instead. I was getting good at knowing how to get what I wanted with him. Next up—a raise.

Antonio typed at lightning speed, even if he didn't use the correct fingers. It was kinda cute. He was working hard on reports for our latest cases we were wrapping

up. He really loved his job and was a hardworking dude.
I liked that about him. We worked well together too. I'm
not sure becoming fuck buddies wouldn't change that.

He looked up from his computer screen. "Ky, you get
them notes from Mr. Cleo? I need them for this report."

"Oh yeah, I'll go over there and remind him." I looked
at the big clock on the wall and knew it was close to
Jacques's last client wrap up.

I walked briskly down the hall and knocked lightly. He
cracked the door with a smile.

"Hey, Jacques, you busy? Did you get a chance to do a
reading on the Gordon and Mao Dae Kim fraud case that
Vince gave you?"

"Hey, Kylie," he smiled warmly.

I bit my bottom lip. "We kinda need it . . . like today."

"Yes, yes. Let me grab my notes that I typed up." He
started ruffling papers on his desk until he found the
folder. "What I got is that it was definitely an inside job.
The ringleader was Mao, the guy your client suspects. But
he didn't work alone. He came up with the plan to have a
fall and promised the guys who helped lie for him some
cut of the lawsuit money. Looks like two men on his team
were in on it."

"This is great, Jacques. I'll pass it on to Antonio."

"That's it?"

"Yup, that's it. We just needed confirmation before we
moved forward. Listen, we know you're busy, Jacques.
Just invoice us, and I'll bring the check over. I'm so
happy Vince knows your work and is a believer. I think
having you as a consultant is taking Like a Fly on the
Wall up a notch."

"Why, thanks, Kylie. I'll email you my notes now."

I started to leave, then Jacques said, "Hey, hey, slow down. How's it going over there? I don't see you as much anymore. Your energy seems a little scattered."

"It does? Well, I guess that's because it is," I sighed. "Sometimes, I feel like what I'm doing is causing more harm than good. Don't you?"

Jacques leaned against the wall. "How so?"

"I mean, both of us have jobs that help people uncover the truth. I feel like what we're doing helps people. Then a part of me is like . . . What is the freakin' point?"

"Why? Because they stay with the person that cheated?"

"Well, yes, in some cases, but it seems like they hire us just to win, you know? They are in a fight to be right. Like they pay us to get proof when they already know the truth. Like this new client we have. Her husband knows she's a ho already. Like you *really* need us to follow her?"

We laughed.

"Kylie, you know people just like confirmation. Sometimes their mates do things so out of character that it's hard to believe. They think they are hallucinating or paranoid, so they come to us to find out. But I get how it can be frustrating. I've had plenty of people in verbally, emotionally, and physically abusive relationships and *still* stay."

"Yeah, so they can freakin' destroy their lives." I threw my hands up.

"Well, one might look at it that way, but there is a pact our souls make to experience certain things that could be a karmic lesson."

"We've seen people who have contracted numerous diseases from a spouse that they *know* they didn't have before and still wanna find out if they're cheating. I'm mean, come oooon, maaaan. Just leave and report that jerk to CDC. Who the hell would sign up for that kind of Karma?"

"Self-esteem and mental illness play a big role too, you know. Everyone has their journey, Kylie. That's why I team up with therapists and various healers since some things are out of my scope. I have a nice referral list. What's really going on, Kylie? Talk to me."

God, I felt like he could see right through me. I wondered if he knew I did something wrong. "Sorry, I know I'm being a Debbie Downer. It's this new case I got. It's really messing with me."

"Which one, the wife you're following?"

"It's just something we expect more from a man. To see a woman doing it-it just—"

"Wow, that just sexist," Jacques said with a sly grin.

I giggled. "Whatever."

"You would need popcorn if you were listening in on some of the sessions I have with my clients who are women and who cheat . . . a lot."

"Yeah, I know we cheat, but we do it more for revenge or lack of love, not usually just to get our rocks off."

Jacques took a deep breath and tilted his head. "I sense a lot of tension with this case. It's not everything you think it's about."

"Yeah, I'm wondering if there is more to the story since the husband is so obsessed. I think he just gets turned on from the reports. Some people are sick like that. I think we got enough proof. It's like he always wanted more."

"Just keep your eyes open."

"What? Why?"

"Nothing crazy. Can't put my finger on it. Just protect your energy daily, so you don't let your work bring you down. I can see it's already affecting you, Kylie. I'll send you some meditations to do."

***

We were startled by two hard bangs, and then the door swung open. "Hey, hey . . . What up? What up?" It was Hicham, Jacques's obnoxious little brother.

His eyes went to my lips and then my eyes. "There she goes again. Movie star. Heeeey, gorgeous."

He opened his arms for a hug, and I gave him a quick one with a pat on the back. He looked different than I remembered him. He had dark circles under his eyes and looked like he aged like five years. Too much partying, I bet. I'm sure Mackenzie would diagnose him in two minutes. She would definitely make him get a cleanse. I learned from her that dark circles meant kidney or liver issues. He was a sharp dresser, though, and also smelled nice. I'll give him that. He looked like he was about to step into a music video.

"'Sup? You ready? I'm hungry as hell." His voice was scratchy like he had been yelling at a concert.

Jacques was calm and always seemed to be like a father figure to Hicham, who was off-the-chain-hyper all the time. He was reading a text and slowly walking back into his office. "Give me a moment. I have a client I need to call back to reschedule. Excuse me for a minute."

Hicham shooed him off. "You go 'head and make your call." He stretched his arm around my shoulder. "I'ma get reacquainted with this sweeeet, fine, Nubian princess over here."

I slowly took his arm off of me. "Oh, stop it. You're such a flirt," I snickered.

Jacques peeked his head out of the door and said, "Hey, hey, please, leave Kylie alone." He shook his head.

Hicham was a little bit cuter when I met him months before, definitely not as fine as Jacques, but nice looking. He had nice big eyes and long eyelashes—I guess it came from the Italian side—and he had the same gentle smile as Jacques. I wonder how hard it was for him growing up with such a fine brother. He's gotta have a lot of insecurities. I think that is what he was overcompensating for with his overly aggressive tactics. He was harmless, though—more of a one-man comedy show than anything else.

"He's fine, Jacques. I can handle myself. I know kick-boxing." I pretended to block and duck blows.

Jacques laughed. "Hey, Kylie, are you done with work? Wanna join us for dinner? We're just going down the block. Cheesecake Factory in CocoWalk."

"Daaaamn, Cheesecake Factory? My weakness. I . . . I don't know, I gotta—"

Jacques spoke into his cell, "Yes, good evening, Phyllis. How are you?" He pointed as if he'd be right back and went into his office and left us in the waiting room. Hicham sat down and patted the seat next to him, so I joined him.

He whispered and leaned in a bit too familiar. I could smell his cologne even stronger. But all his scents together made an interesting combo: cologne, a hint of weed mixed with spearmint gum breath.

"Yo, Kylie . . . I didn't want to blow you up in front of Jacques since he speaks so highly of you, but you acted like you ain't even know me the other day."

"What do you mean?"

"I did not know that you got down like thaaaat." His eyes widened, and he shook his head in amazement. "But your secret's safe with me."

I lurched back. "Huh? Get down like whaaaat? What are you talking about, crazy?" I chuckled nervously. My heart started to beat fast. Did I send him signals? Did he think I was flirting? I was lost.

"Kylie . . . I was *there*. I saw you. Come on. How long you gonna play this little game? It's cute and all, but I saw you spread-eagle at that club." I gulped. Hicham's eyes were cold. "You and old boy were getting it iiiin." He softened his voice and smiled as he remembered. "Then you had like some girls and another dude groping at you. I was about to ask if I could get a piece of the action."

My stomach churned, and I felt sweat beads forming on my forehead. I put my finger to my lips and said in a panicked whisper, "Stop. Can you please stop? Look, I don't remember. I was drugged. I ate a weed brownie by accident . . . but it was a mistake. A huge mistake." My heart thumped so loudly in my chest. The embarrassment took over. "I don't remember much of . . . anything."

He covered his mouth as if he were about to laugh. Then Hicham leaned back in his chair and folded his hands across his stomach. "Edibles? Kylie! For real? That's a weak excuse. You were *not* blacked out. I heard you coming like a porn star. You were wide awake, enjoying yourself. Come oooon, brownies don't make you do what *you* was doing. I've had edibles before."

"I ate the *whole* thing, Hicham. I was only supposed to eat like one-fourth. I don't do drugs. I wasn't used to it."

"You don't have to explain, baby. It's okay if you got a little wild side." He shook his head and licked his lips, looking at my legs. He rubbed my knee and then patted it. I flinched.

I tapped my foot nervously. "Hicham, please. Please, don't say anything to Jacques. Please. It's still freaking me out."

"But why were you there? That's not a place for people who don't like to fuck."

"We were on a surveillance job. We were doing a job."

"Y'all was on your job, all right. Shit, I need to work there. You taking any applications? I got a mean stroke game."

He laughed, and it made me feel so disgusted. Cheap. Uneasy. Like a piece of meat. Hicham saw me naked. He saw my legs opened. He saw me doing unspeakable things. I was so humiliated. I wanted to hit him for making light of the situation.

It was *not*.

Fucking

Funny.

Hicham softened his tone and smiled softly. "Look, I won't say anything to Jacques, but let me take you out while I'm here. Let's get to know each other better."

The sly grin on his face pissed me off. "I do not want to lead you on. I'm not like that, Hicham. I really am *not* that chick. I was literally hallucinating." I lowered my voice to a whisper. "I'm so embarrassed. I still can't believe it happened."

His eyes focused on my lips as I talked. He bit his bottom lip. He had a look of obsession like he could remember me naked. Thank God they didn't allow phones. He would have definitely taken photos of me. Then I remembered Antonio's spy glasses. Shit. I sure hoped I didn't end up in the evidence pile.

Jacques's door squeaked open, and I shook my head at Hicham, so he would keep his trap shut. Hicham mouthed, "You good, you good, ma," as he patted my leg again and put his arm around my shoulders like we were best buds. My stomach squirmed. I don't know why, but I had a bad feeling about all of this.

Jacques walked out. Thank God I was saved. He said, "Wow, that Phyllis tries to keep me on the phone forever. She was just booking an appointment but wanted to give me all kinds of updates on her cat and grandson. Sweet lady, but maaaan." He dropped his head back and smiled. Jacques pointed back and forth to us. "But what's going on *here?*" He tilted his head to the side at me, surprised I allowed Hicham so close to me.

Hicham slowly moved his hand from behind my neck. "Oh, nothing. We just catching up. We were trying to talk low since you were on the phone. And Kylie will be joining us for dinner." He looked at me and smiled as if he dared me to reject the offer. This motherfucker . . .

"Really?" Jacques smiled.

I nodded. "Sure, I'm *very* hungry. I can input the rest of my reports in the morning. We haven't hung out in a minute anyhow." I sighed as I surrendered.

"Oh, I already sent off that report to you and Antonio."

"Cool, thank you."

Hicham clapped his hands. "Great. It's a date with two handsome brothers. Let's get it in." He winked at me.

"Kylie isn't like that. Come on, have some respect, man."

"Hey, she might surprise you."

"Your jokes are always soooo out of line. Have a little respect for my friends, please." Jacques got his key and opened the door for us to leave so he could lock up.

"I don't pay him any mind." I rolled my eyes.

Jacques looked at me with apologetic eyes, and I just waved him off as if to say, "Don't worry about it." He said, "Let's go, guys."

I loved how he defended my honor, but if he only knew the truth, I would lose all of his respect. "I'll be right back. Lemme go get my purse and sweater. It's freezing in there sometimes. Antonio can lock up the agency."

"Ooooh, that's your coworker's name? I thought it was Will or something."

I cut my eyes at Hicham. *Shut. The. Fuck. Up.* I doubted he could make it through the night without saying anything. He was being a real asshole now. I didn't know how I'd get through this dinner without punching him.

I walked back into the office while the guys headed to the elevator. Antonio was on the phone when I walked in, and he smiled at me as he paced around the office.

Earlier, he had on a landscaper's outfit since he was on surveillance in the morning. He had changed into jeans, nice black shoes, and a black shirt with a few buttons opened. I watched him pace around and play with the blinds in the window. He was a really nice-looking guy. Well, let's face it; he was *fionnne*. He probably wouldn't be single for long. Maybe he had a date, who knows?

I suddenly got hit with a flashback of him on top of me, sucking my nipples. He was talking shit while he did it too . . . *"You watching me? Are you watching?"* I saw a flicker of his tongue, his eyes staring into mine. His big hands were exploring my body, manhandling me. We were kissing. He was a good kisser too. I enjoyed it. My body suddenly got hot. I had to shake it off.

I took a deep breath and quickly got my purse and sweater. These flashbacks were too much. Oh my Gawd, I almost fucked *Antonio*. Clearly, there had been a lot of pent-up energy between us these last few months.

I wrote on Post-it Note for him. *"Check email. Jacques sent report. I'm gonna text you."*

He covered the phone and whispered, "I'm on the phone with a client. Okay, hit me up."

I made it over to the elevator with the guys and texted him.

Kylie: I'm going to kill you. smh

Antonio: What I do now?

Kylie: How come you didn't tell me that Jacques's brother, Hicham, was at Charlie's Den with us? OMG, I could fucking die. He told me he saw me.

Antonio: Oh shit, that is who that guy was? Remember, I said a dude knew you? He said your name. I couldn't place a face with a name.

Kylie: Yes. Well, he is rubbing it in my face now. It's so embarrassing. I still can't believe all of that really happened.

Antonio: You want me to fuck him up? Lol

Kylie: No, I can handle him, I think.

Antonio: Calling you.

Kylie: Don't. I'm with him and Jacques. We off to dinner. Hicham told me when Jacques wasn't in the room.

Antonio: Oh . . . Okaaaay. You so damn dramatic. You had a good time. It's called living, baby. Next time, noooo brownie. I want you to remember everything.

Kylie: Next time, eh?

Antonio: You read right, woman. (wink)

Kylie: I . . . hate . . . you . . .

Antonio: I know. You ain't say that last night, though. You loved me. LMFAO

Kylie: Goodbye, jerk.

Antonio: Chiiiiill, li'l mama. Just jokes. You'll be all right, my little drama queen.

Kylie: I know. K, gotta run. Ciao.

Antonio: Enjoy. I'll call you later.

It was a cool night, and Grand Street was sprinkled with a few tourists buying from vendors. Jacques, Hicham, and I took a stroll down the block to The Cheesecake Factory. I hoped some emotional eating of pasta and bread would help me forget my porn star moment of recklessness.

Chapter 13

Jacques

The Cheesecake Factory was a full house, and I really didn't like crowds, but I would grin and bear it. What made it worse was the energy at my own table. Dinner with these two was beyond awkward. I keep catching strange glances between Hicham and Kylie, and I think I must be paranoid or something. I mean, it's not even possible. Couldn't be. It has to be in my mind.

He sat next to her, and they were both across from me. They seemed almost as if they were on a date. I couldn't see them fooling around, though. It just doesn't even make logical sense. He is not her type. Kylie was being overly friendly to Hicham, but it looked forced. Maybe she was trying to be nice on my behalf? Very puzzling.

"Soooo, how long you gonna eat bird food? What's the length of this program you on?" Hicham asked me.

"It's not bird food, and for the rest of my life, I'd like to have a plant-based diet if I can do it. And for your information, I'm eating healthy, and I have more food than you. Look at this . . . rigatoni with roasted eggplant, peppers, broccoli, olives, and a big salad." I kissed my fingers, imitating an Italian. "This is good. How do you come to Cheesecake and order a cheeseburger?" I looked at Kylie and shook my head.

"I know, right?" Kylie scoffed.

"'Cause they shit be good." Hicham laughed and took a big exaggerated bite.

Kylie laughed. "They do make everything good. I don't think I've ever had a dish here I didn't like."

Hicham dipped his French fry in ketchup and said, "Maaaan, I can't hate, 'cause whatever you doing, it's working. You look solid. I ain't never seen you look like you an athlete and shit. No homo," he laughed.

"Yeah, Jacques, you do look good," she winked at me.

"Hey, you making me jealous." Hicham playfully cut his eyes at Kylie as he stuffed a French fry in his mouth.

"Hicham, please. You have enough confidence for *everyone* in the room. I can't see you ever being jealous," she laughed.

He offered her a sip of his drink, and she declined. Hicham gave me this strange, puckered lips look, pointing to my phone on the table and raising his eyebrows. I looked at my cell and realized I had a missed text message he sent ten minutes ago.

Hicham: Can you leave us alone for a little?

Jacques: No, for what?

Hicham: Come on, I'm feeling a vibe. Let me at least try. Just go to the office real quick and come back and get us in like a half?

He looked into Kylie's eyes. "You right. I'm not the jealous type. I just really like you. You cool peoples. I think what you do is pretty fascinating too—spying on motherfuckers? That's gotta be fun. Let me interview you for my blog or something. I can probably get the magazine to feature it too. People love stories about private investigators. It might get y'all a lot of publicity."

"Wow? Really?"

I chimed in. "You know, that's not a bad idea, Hicham. I know your audience will love the whole cheaters' angle too."

Kylie said, "Well, I'm down, but I have to ask my boss, Vince, first. I'm sure he's gonna want to put in his two cents. I'm still pretty new and far from an official PI, but I do have some good stories already." She was eager to share.

I said, "Like Vince will say no. You know Vince loves attention. This would be nationwide publicity for Like a Fly on the Wall."

"You're so right, and I can plug you too while I'm at it, since you work with us, Jacques."

Hicham leaned in closer to Kylie. He was so aggressive it was embarrassing. "Ah, seeee, now you're talking. You know I gotta show big bro some love. You and I gotta get up before I leave so I can interview you." He gave me this look to get lost. I ignored him.

She shrugged. "Sure. I can do that."

I said, "Kylie, it would be great exposure for you. They have a lot of subscribers."

"Yes, over 1 million," Hicham chimed in.

"Damn, well, in that case . . ."

"Oh, come on. You doubt me?"

"No, not at all, but I had no idea there were that many people. So, how long you in town?" Kylie asked him while stirring her iced tea.

"How long you want me in town?"

Kylie giggled. "You are a trip. Can you be serious for once?"

I know it's weird, but I was a bit jealous. I did not like Hicham invading on our friendship. He was always starved for attention growing up, even though he got a lot of it from Mom. When it came to friends, he went above and beyond to fit in. Now, he's using his magazine exposure as a way to win Kylie over. She's a smart girl, though. She and Hicham . . . I won't allow it. I mean, it's just wrong. He'll destroy her.

***

"Excuse me, y'all. Be right back." Hicham went to the bathroom, and I figured now was my chance.

"So, what's this buddy-buddy thing going on with you and my brother?" I know I sounded jealous, but I couldn't take it back.

She laughed. "What? Oh, please, I'm just being nice. He's not as much of a jerk as I thought."

"Really, Kylie? Don't fall for it."

"Oh, what do you mean . . . me and Hicham?" She looked back to make sure he didn't hear her. "No, no, Jacques, he is soooo *not* my type. I'm not going there. We'll do the interview, and that's it. He is definitely determined and keeps trying. I'm a big girl. I can handle him."

The tension in my shoulders subsided. "Okay, he does have the Berradi charm still. He might reel you in with his magical smoothness." I tilted my head to the side.

"Yeah . . . I highly doubt that. He doesn't do it for me." She giggled nervously and lurched back. "Hold up. Jacques, are *you* jealous?"

I felt my face flush. "No, no. Come on; you're like my family now. I'm just looking out for you."

She tilted her head and rested her hand on mine. "Thanks, Jacques, you're so sweet."

When she touched my hand, I saw a white flicker in her eyes, and she suddenly had a layer of another face over hers. It was happening again. The same hologram type vision I had when I saw Dee transform into Saasha. This time, the face was of a gentle 50-something-year-old white lady. I saw her with a guitar and felt a rush of warm memories come at me.

The woman was a musician and wrote songs mainly about injustice and love. She was full of passion. I guess she was an activist in her day. Maybe a hippie. I heard my guides say, *"Kylie has come back to help others in love. She has a bigger mission than she knows."*

"Jacques? Jacques?" The face vanished, and Kylie's eyes returned and stared at me with furrowed brows. "You good?"

"Wow, umm . . . sorry. I just saw one of your—"

"One of my what? Did you get a vision? OMG, do tell." She leaned in for details.

"I saw you as an older white lady, long brown hair . . . a musician. It felt so nice. So familiar. Like we were—"

"What?"

I didn't want to admit it, but she was my wife. "We were close . . . cousin, but maybe sister, not sure. Felt like family."

"That quick you got that?"

"It comes to me as instant memory now. I wasn't even in meditation trying to get it."

"Whaaaat . . . We gotta find out. How cool is that? A musician, huh? That sounds right . . . why I love music so much."

"Yeah, I don't know if it's cool. I'd rather have more control of it. Something is happening to me. It seems like when I am close to someone or if they touch me, I see their past life. It's like a film. Like someone is projecting onto your face." I put my hands in front of her face to show her how close it was.

"Like a hologram?"

"Yes, exactly . . . exactly. Only I can see them in 3D. I see the features clearly, and I feel their energy and remember their lives in an instant."

"You might be developing a new superpower or something. You're like a *mutant* from *X-Men*. You're mutating." Kylie started laughing hysterically, and I joined her.

"Stop it."

"Soooo . . . Was I pretty? My hologram? Was I hot?"

"Yes, very. A big heart. Almost angelic. Calming. I guess that's why we got close so fast. Our souls knew each other already."

"Yes, we are definitely like fam. We gotta do a reading one day to find out why we connected. Maybe your psychic homie Melissa can do it and find out more."

"I would be open to that. There's always a reason." I kissed her hand and smiled. "I'm so happy you are my friend. I do want to thank you for being there for me. I know it's not easy being a friend to someone like me."

Hicham walked back in from the bathroom just as I let go of her hand.

"Well, would you look at this shit. Just like my brother. I walk away for five minutes, and you already pushing up on my girl."

Kylie sucked her teeth. "What? Your girl? Hicham, please, get a grip."

"I'm just playing with y'all, all right, Kylie? I wanna get your number so that we can plan for the interview. I wanna prepare my questions and all." He handed his cell to her to plug in her number.

My heart flipped. I feel so weird that I couldn't put my finger on it. I just have a bad feeling about them connecting further. Maybe I was just a tad jealous and paranoid. But Kylie is a smart girl. She's right. She can handle him.

I ignored Hicham's texts asking me to leave them alone. When the bill came, I paid for it, and I knew I would hear his mouth all the way home.

Chapter 14

Kylie

The next evening, I went to dinner with Hicham to be interviewed, or so he said. He seemed slightly drunk and high the second I showed up. What a turnoff. How unprofessional too.

We were seated in a dark corner. I took a deep breath and looked around at the restaurant. It was pretty romantic. Low blue lights and soft music. He really thought we were on a date.

Hicham looked at me with dreamy eyes. "Whatchu be thinking about, Kylie?" He was so corny.

"Oh, nothing. This place is nice. You've come here before?"

"Nah, but it had good reviews. I thought we need a chill spot to talk and get to know each other."

"Yeah, okay, you mean to do the interview?"

"You ever thought about modeling? I would love to shoot you. You have such great bone structure and your hair . . . You just have such an earthy look that I'm sure I could capture."

"Yes, I've thought about it, but it's hard to model. It's like acting, and I suck at it."

"Just be your natural self."

"Who would I model for?"

"Me, my portfolio. I would add you to my website. Who knows, you might get discovered. Natural is in now. The gigs I'm in town for are already cast, and I know you wouldn't want to do what they're doing anyway," he laughed.

"Oh Gawd, what is it? Porn?"

"No, not at all. It's models painted with henna and done topless. It doesn't look topless, though. That's the beauty of it. It's a campaign for a new nightclub."

"Yeah, I'm good." I shook my head and puffed up the back of my 'fro with my fingers. "I appreciate the offer, though."

"One day, I am going to shoot you. One day," he pointed at me.

Someone was walking around the restaurant handing out flowers to the ladies. A man offered me one, and I declined.

"This is a date night spot, you know?"

"So, what's wrong with that? Am I not your type? Why do you seem so uncomfortable around me? I'm a good dude." He tapped his chest.

"Uncomfortable? That's in your mind, Hicham. I'm just still embarrassed about what . . . what I did. What you saw. It's so crazy. It's not like me at all. I think you have the wrong idea about me."

He moved his seat closer to the table and spoke softer. "Well, let me tell you something, Kylie. You could be a star in a movie. You are just so unbelievably sexy. To hear you moaning . . . You had so many chicks jealous. They wanted a piece of the action. *Everyone* was looking at you."

"That makes me feel much better." I shook my head and folded my arms. I felt naked.

The food we ordered arrived, and he was trying so hard to be sexy even when eating. Tartar sauce got on his finger, and he licked it off seductively. I was grossed out.

He continued, "It was wild. You had like four people on you. That shit musta felt gooood."

I was scared to ask him, but I did. "So, what were you doing all that time you could watch me so much?"

"I was fucking. What do you think?" He laughed. "But while I was hitting it, I was looking at you. No disrespect but . . ." His glare was intense, and he reached out his hand, pretending to grab me, "You have like the most perfect breasts. Not too big, not too small. Not that they could ever be too big."

"All right, already, what is the purpose of this meeting? You said you wanted to interview me, not keep bringing this shit up. I'm over it now."

"Whoa, whoa. Be easy, Princess, and let's be clear. *You* brought it up. I just wanted to get to know you first. Is that all right?" He touched my chin and then took out his iPad. "Okay, we can start with the interview now since you getting all touchy. You mind if I record you?"

"No." I released a sigh of relief since, at this point, I just wanted to get it over with. I tried to look at the bright side of the benefit of exposure the agency would get. I would take one for the team. This "interview/date" was grueling, however.

"So, what's the most fulfilling part of your job?"

"I enjoy helping people find the truth so that they are not taken advantage of anymore. Our team specializes in uncovering liars. People who are taking advantage of others. Our workload goes from basic insurance fraud cases to infidelity."

"What trends do you see the most?"

"Well, in many cases, people are using social media to cheat. Whether they are using dating apps or just reuniting with old classmates on Facebook, cheating seems to be at an all-time high. Statistics show men and women between the ages of 40 to 49 cheat the most. Men over 60 as well. Also, women are not the only victims. We have many cases where the men are being cheated on."

"Real talk. I'm happy about that. Men always get the short end of the stick when women are sneaky as fuck."

"Yeah, we're just smarter. Most of the male clients leave too much of a paper trail. They have long relationships on text. They are very sloppy and make my job easy. The women are usually a tad harder to catch," I laughed.

"Is your goal to be a full-time private eye? To help save people from broken relationships?"

"Yes, I'd love to. That's definitely a goal. It's a very fulfilling job helping people find out the truth. It could be dangerous if caught, but I'm learning to be careful."

"Careful, how? You ever blow your cover?"

"No, just a few close calls, though. It could get messy. If you act too suspicious, if someone notices you following them or listening to them . . . you know? But since I'm still new, I don't do that much surveillance. I do more online digging, which suits me well since I'm naturally nosy."

The waiter came with more food, and Hicham paused the recording.

"Most women are nosy."

I laughed. "True."

He wrinkled his nose and looked deep into my eyes. "I just see how protective Jacques is of you, and now I know why. You're kinda special, Kylie. I mean that in a good way—you good people. I'm just trying to see what kind of girl you really are . . . Since he don't really know."

"Look, your brother and I are cool. We're just friends. We've all been through a lot in these last few months, and he's had my back, and I've had his."

"Oh, so y'all never fucked? Like ever?" He looked at me with accusing eyes. They squinted, and he pursed up his lips.

"Hell no. We are strictly platonic. We never even held hands."

"Okaaaay, so if he wanted to change that, you . . . you wouldn't say yes?" He raised an eyebrow.

I gulped my drink and lied. "No, no, we're friends. But why does that even matter to you?" I was fed up with his line of questioning. "Where is this going?" Talk about awkward.

"'Cause if you and I go that route, I don't want to worry about you cheating on me with my bro."

The audacity of this fool.

"How are you even thinking it's going *there?*"

His face flushed, and he seemed shocked at my rejection. "I'ma be right back." He got up in a rush and went to the restroom. I guess he had a bladder problem. He was always in the damn bathroom.

He took a long while, almost fifteen minutes or so. When he came back, it was like he was another person. He had an intense glare. He clapped his hands loudly. "Okay, Kylie. Let's wrap up this article so we can hurry up and get out of here." He licked his lips.

I chuckled. "Yeah, right. We're just meeting about this article, and you pretty much are bribing me to do it." I pointed to his chest and mine. "You and I *won't* be happening."

"Why not?" He lowered his voice. "You were giving that pussy up, girl. Motherfuckers were all over you."

"What's your problem? Why you being so disrespectful?"

"You keep treating me like a sucka. You know how many chicks would jump at *this* opportunity?" He pointed to his dick. "You keep playing all innocent. Come on, Kylieeee. I know the *real* you. I know you remember seeing me."

My voice was low and trembled at his dark transformation. "I told you already that I don't remember anything." My heart was beating fast, and my hands were shaking slightly. He was not in his right mind.

He sat next to me. "Let me make you feel good." He spoke low in my ear. "You won't regret it, I promise. I'm a little high right now, but I know if I fuck you, *I'll* remember everything. I will pound that pussy just right. I want you so badly. Let's get out of here."

I was paralyzed. I wanted him to get away from me. I wanted to scream, but I didn't want to make a scene or make him react. He put his hand on my neck and crawled his fingers into my hair. I jerked back. "Okaaaay, that's it, Hicham, get off of me. You've gone too far. You are delusional. I'm done. Please move."

He stared in my face with a stupid smile as if he thought this were all a joke. "What?" he laughed. "I thought you liked it. I saw them pulling your hair. Sighs of ecstasy would come out when they pulled your hair." He closed his eyes and shook his head, remembering. "It was beautiful."

My voice quivered. "Get off of me." I shoved him. "I've had enough of you disrespecting me. We're done." He cornered me in the booth. Then he got closer to my face. I tried to get up. "We're done. Please move so I can leave."

A waiter came over. "Is everything okay?"

"No, no, it is *not* okay. I want to leave, but he won't get up."

Hicham jumped up. "Quit being a fuckin' baby. You're free to go. But let's talk." He threw a hundred-dollar bill on the table and followed me out.

"Kylie! Kylie!" he yelled.

I raced away from him, trying to remain calm. He continued. "What's wrong with me? Why don't you like me? I was just joking with you. You way too sensitive to be a chick from Brooklyn. What, you don't like light-skinned brothers? You on that fight-the-power shit?" He threw his fist up in the air and laughed. "What? You need you a dark Mandingo motherfucker with dreadlocks?"

My blood boiled now, and I wanted to body slam him to the ground. If he weren't so tall, I probably could fling his frail frame. At this point, I didn't give a shit anymore.

"First of all, Hicham, you are *Italian and French*. That's *Caucasian*. You ain't light-skinned and hardly a 'brother.'" I did air quotes that must have infuriated him even more. I kept walking toward the parking lot to my car. I looked back and saw he was on my heels.

"Who told you that? That's not true."

I stopped in my tracks and spewed my words with such malice. "Hicham, for *real?* Are you that drunk or high that you forgot that I was there helping Jacques with your mom's journals? I know all about that affair your mother had with the Italian man—Benny. How could you forget that? You are fucking *delusional*. Go home. Leave me alone."

He grabbed my arm. "Stop it, yo, Kylie. Shut the fuck up. Shut up. You real funny. *Real* funny. It's women like you that get on my nerves. You just like my mother. Got your nose all up in the air. You're disrespectful but swear you Miss Prim and Proper, like yo' shit don't stink. Yes, you that same whore who will fuck all the homies." I shook him off of me. The waiter was by the door watching. "That same bitch that will let niggas run a train on that ass and have a bunch of lesbians feeling up your tits."

People started to stare and whisper. I was mortified.

My eyes cringed. "You are one unstable motherfucker. How could you be Jacques's brother? You got the baaaad part of the gene pool. You are bat shit crazy. And guess what? You can tell Jacques everything, everythaaaang since I don't care anymore." My voice cracked. "I don't give a fuck. I have a lot to tell him myself. One more minute with you is not even worth it. You are an insensitive, narcissistic asshole. *Fuck you, Hicham. Fuck your article and fuck you.*" My eyes started to water. I couldn't get to my car fast enough. I pressed the alarm on my car, and just as I opened the door, he rushed up behind me.

"You forgot something." His eyes were glazed. "I need my good night kiss. I'm sorry." He pinned me up against the car and grabbed my face. "Let me make it up to you."

I yanked away, and he forced my face to his and stuck his tongue in my mouth. His breath stunk of vodka. I fought him off and wiped my mouth. He grabbed my wrists tightly and pressed up on me again.

I was petrified. "Hicham, get the fuck off of me. I'm going to scream, and you're going to get arrested. People are looking at us. Do you *really* want to go to jail?" My voice was quivering now. My heart raced.

Hicham's eyes shone like glass. "Damn, your lips are soft. Don't worry about people. You like when they watch, don't you? I saw it with my own eyes. That gets your pussy wet." He tugged on my hair and pressed his body up on mine with brutal force. I felt his hardness in his pants. I tried to push him off of me, but I felt so weak. My hands shook. "Come on, Kylie. Stop playing hard to get. You know you wanna get fucked tonight."

"I'm going to ask you one last time." My voice was steady and low. "Get the fuck away from me before I call the cops."

"I'm not gonna hurt you. Just pretend you on them brownies again."

I hit his shoulder, but he didn't move. His leg was in between mine, and he held me against my car. Although he was so slim, his strength was startling. I only had one weapon—my knee.

I kneed him in the balls as hard as I could.

He curled over, and his voice went up an octave. "You fucking bitch! What is *wrong* with you?" His eyes were red, and I saw no sense of sanity left in them. Whatever he was on completely took over him.

My voice cracked. "I warned you to get the fuck off of me." I jumped in my car and locked the doors.

He started pacing around my car and laughing uncontrollably and yelling, "See this lady right here. She's a whore who loves her pussy eaten in front of a hundred people. Whore! Whore! Fucking whore." I was humiliated. People on their way to dinner watched us as they exited their cars. Tears streamed down my face as I fumbled with the car key. I couldn't get it into the ignition. My hands were shaking uncontrollably now. I saw him walk away back into the restaurant, and I breathed a deep sigh of relief and called Jacques.

"Jacques, your brother is crazy. He just attacked me! He's out of his mind. He needs help."

"Wait. What? Slow down. What happened? Where are you? Still at the—"

"Hicham assaulted me." I started crying harder, as it all hit me. I sobbed. "He held me against my car and stuck his tongue in my mouth. He pinned me down. I'm so scared."

"Oh my God, where are you? Calm down. Calm down. I don't understand."

"Bone Fish Grill on Biscayne Blvd. We met for the interview, so he said. He-he's crazy. Hicham's gonna rape someone if he hasn't already. He's unstable. He really needs to be on meds. I think he's high on something—something bad."

"Are you serious? You want me to come there? Where is he now?"

"No, no. He left . . . I think."

"Okay, come to my house then."

"Hell no. He's probably on his way to your house. I don't ever want to be in the same room with his psychotic ass again."

"Okay, meet me at the office."

As I started the car, it began shaking violently. I looked behind me. Hicham was on the bumper, moving the vehicle as if he were trying to pick it up. It was shifting as if he could do it too! This couldn't be really happening. He came toward the passenger side and started banging on the window. "Where you going? Let me in, Kylie. Let me iiiin. I'm sorry. Let me talk to you. Open the door."

My throat was dry and tight. I grasped the wheel. "Oh my God, Jacques. He's trying to break my window."

My stomach was in knots, and I put my foot on the gas so hard, I could drive off. He was holding on and running with my car until I picked up the pace.

"Jacques, are you still there? Are you there?"

"Yes, yes. I'm on my way."

"He was just shaking my car. He was holding the car like he thought he could stop it. You gotta get down here and get him. He's on something."

Chapter 15

Jacques

I could hear it in her voice. Kylie was terrified. I felt helpless. I got in my car immediately and kept her on the phone.

"Was there something else going on? Did you possibly lead him on in any way?"

"Fuck, no, Jacques. Are you serious? Now it's *my* fault for this sick behavior? Did you *not* hear me? He was running with the car, shaking my car. Who the fuck does that? Like he thought he had superhuman strength or something."

"No, no, I'm not justifying his behavior, but I have to say you two have been acting a tad bit friendlier than usual. I know you didn't like him before, so I thought it was strange."

Her car was in front of our office building when I got there. She embraced me tightly and sobbed in my arms. "Kylie, it's okay, it's okay. I'm here."

We walked into the empty building and spoke in the lobby. Her eyes were red from crying and with sunken shoulders, she said, "Listen, about him and me being extra friendly . . . I didn't want him to tell you something. I was embarrassed, and I'm still in shock that it happened. He was holding the information over my head so that I would be nice to him."

My heart was tight. The anticipation in the air was thick. I tilted my head to the side, trying to brace myself for the news.

"I had to do a surveillance job at a-an exclusive swingers' spot on South Beach."

My eyebrows went up. "Oh, really?"

"Yes, and by mistake, I ate one of Mackenzie's edible brownies before I got there. I got extremely high and did some things I do not even remember."

"What? Are you serious? That's pretty scary."

"Well, Hicham was there."

I felt a blow to my belly. "You and him?"

"No, no, thank God. He was just watching. But it was Antonio and—"

My chest heaved. "Woooow, really? Antonio?" I smiled since I figured they would connect eventually. They did have a special chemistry.

"We didn't go aaaall the way. But from what he and Hicham said, I was definitely out of character."

I tried to keep a look of concern on my face and not let my mind wonder about what "out of character" really was. Not my sweet Kylie. I started to get aroused, picturing her having sex with various men.

"Jacques, your brother is on something serious. I don't know much about drugs, but I think its coke. Or maybe that YK or bath salts, but it's something crazy 'cause he lost his shit. He kept going to the bathroom all night. He was acting so strange. He is a danger to society." Her hands went up in the air as she reenacted how he pushed her.

"He pressed up against me and was damn near choking me with his tongue. I was so afraid he would hit me. I don't ever want to be around him again. And he has so much rage about your mother. He kept comparing me to her, how I was just like her. How women lie. He has some serious fucking issues. It was like he was taking out everything on *me*. He was also mad at me since I told him he was white. He's in denial."

She started crying. "I didn't want you to think bad about me."

"Kylie, nothing can change our friendship. I know your soul. I'm just so sorry that happened to you." I clenched my jaws. "Let me go deal with my brother. He's not going to do that ever again." I put my hand on her shoulder. "Do you want to press charges?"

"No, no. I wouldn't do that, but he needs help. He needs like mental help or a rehab—something."

"Let me go find him before he causes any more trouble." I hugged Kylie and walked her to her car. As I sped home, I looked up at the illuminated full moon in the night sky. I called Hicham three more times on the way back to my house. His phone kept going to voicemail, and that was full. I was worried about his state of mind, but I figured he might be home. I got to the condo and saw my front door was ajar.

"Hicham," I screamed.

"Yo, bro, I'm in here." He was in the bathroom.

"You left the front door open. Come out now. What the fuck is going on? You could be in jail right now. Are you fucking crazy putting your hands on a woman? Kylie was scared out of her mind."

He spoke through the door. "Damn, she told you already? Man, she was flirting with me. She's a ho anyhow. I don't know why you keep protecting her. I seen her ass butt naked already."

I sighed. "Yeah, yeah, I know. She told me already."

"Word?" he laughed.

"And it wasn't naked with you. She could easily press charges on you right now. What you did was sexual assault."

I heard the water running.

I shook the knob on the locked door. "Come out here. You gotta get out. Go stay in a hotel. I can't have you in here doing the shit you're doing." I slammed my hand against the door. I was furious, but I really didn't want him to leave. I needed to make sure he didn't get into any more trouble.

Hicham opened the door slowly. His face was dripping from the water, and he was shirtless, drying his face. The smell of vomit permeated my nostrils. I held my nose. He shrugged his shoulders. "Yeah, that dinner ain't agree with me."

"Probably all that shit you got in your system is what that was."

"Yo, Jay, stop wilding over a dramatic ho. I was just giving her a good night kiss. She was flaunting her pussy all night."

"I highly doubt that too. Last I heard—shoving your tongue down an unsuspecting female's mouth is *not* a good night kiss. And what about all the wild shit you were saying to her? She said you kept talking about Mom. You really have to get help. I can't put up with this shit any longer. I'm always cleaning up your mess. I'm sick of it. You're an adult, so stop acting like a bratty teenager."

I saw flashes of him trying to kiss Kylie. I really felt he would rape her if given the opportunity. His spirit was so dark. I looked into his pupils that looked like tiny pinpoints. They were glassy. He was soul-less. His mouth hung open in shock. Hicham's aura was very dark.

"What are you on?"

With hunched shoulders, he lowered his eyes. "Come on, man, I just had a bit too much to drink."

"I'm going to ask you again. *What* are you on?" I stood over him with clenched jaws. I balled my hand into a fist.

My heart was racing with anger. "Don't make me beat it out of you, Hicham. You know *I know* you're lying."

He jerked back, shocked at my aggression. "Come on, man, it's nothing. It's not a big deal, Jay."

I heard a soft whisper from my spirit guides saying. "Go to his room. You'll find the answer."

"Okay, cool. You're not going to tell me? I'll find out for myself." I jogged to the spare room to check his duffle bag and suitcase. I was on my knees, going through his bags. There were several empty bottles of Advil and vitamin cases. I opened the bottles, but the pills didn't look like Advil or vitamins. They were blue. Then I saw a small Ziploc bag of coke hidden in an inside pocket. My heart sank. My head started spinning, and my throat tightened. Marijuana I was used to with him, but what was he doing now? I didn't know what kind of pills they were. No wonder he didn't look like himself.

He stood over me as I held the bottles in my hands and said in a low voice. "It's for depression and headaches. It's nothing. Yo . . . Bro, chill. Why you going through my shit?"

"Hicham, you are a fucking time bomb waiting to explode. Please stop fighting and get help. I'm going to call my client, who is a therapist and a director at a treatment center."

"Yo, you violating for real, now. Fuck outta here, man. I'm not no addict. I don't need no rehab." He laughed. "A treatment center? Yo, I just had a wild night—nothing big."

My jaws tightened, and I gave him a stern glare. "How about this? I will make sure Kylie presses assault charges on you, and you *will* go to jail. And don't even look for me to bail you out."

His voice cracked. "Yo, you would really send me to jail? What the fuck? I just kissed her."

I shook my head and walked away. I had to cool down. I felt defeated. I went into my bedroom and sent a text to my client.

Jacques: Hi, Angela. So sorry to bug you so late. I want to check my brother into your facility.

Angela: Oh no, what is he on?

Jacques: I don't know, but he is high right now. I'm scared he is going to cause harm to others.

Angela: Well, he has to admit himself. You can't force him. Can you talk?

Jacques: No, but I'll step out and call you if it's not too late.

Angela: No, it's fine.

I was in my bedroom for about thirty minutes. I didn't see him, so I knocked on the door. He didn't answer. I hit it again.

He moaned in a groggy voice. "Yo, broooo. I fucked up. I knooow."

"You damn right you fucked up. Come out and let's talk."

"I can't, bro. I fucked up. Mom is gone because of me. I don't even deserve to be here. It's my fault." My heart felt his pain. He cried. "Please, just leave me alone, man. Leave me alone. I wanna just disappear."

I felt a jolt in my stomach. I leaned against the door. "Stop talking crazy." I softened my voice. "Hicham, open the door, please. Why are you talking like that?"

Silence.

"Hicham . . . Hicham." I heard a loud thump. "Hichaaaam!"

I violently shook the door handle. It was locked. I kicked the door open, and he was on the floor. His mouth was open. I screamed and opened one eyelid. He was out cold. Breathing, but not responsive. I reached in my back pocket and called 911. Then I saw an empty bottle of pills on the sink.

Early the next morning, the familiar sound of slow-beeping machines haunted me. The menacing sound brought me back to the worst day of my life . . . the last time I saw my mother alive in the hospital. Hicham lay motionless in the bed. It was disheartening to see him so helpless since he was such a lively spirit.

Hicham had been out of sorts since finding out who his biological father was on top of the tragedy of losing our mom. I figured he was just doing weed and alcohol, more excessive than normal. But clearly, he was dabbling in other drugs. I didn't know the signs of a drug habit, but I knew for sure he was not himself. The counselor assigned to my brother told me the pills he was taking were called Fentanyl, which is also referred to as synthetic heroin. Then they also found coke and alcohol in his system, a dangerous combination. I was furious with him. He knew better, but there was nothing I could do now but wait for him to get healing and counseling.

His eyes rolled back and then slowly turned to me.

"Hicham, you almost died."

"Yeah, I know."

"Don't ever scare me like that again." My chest heaved as I tried to pull it together, but instead, I broke down and started to cry. "I lost Mom, and I can't lose you too." He began to tear up too as I leaned over and hugged him.

"I'm just a fuckup. I'm a burden. But I know . . . I need some help."

"You are *not* a burden. You are an amazing human being. You are a creative genius when you aren't running your mouth." I slapped his hand, and we laughed.

"Your job loves you. You have friends that love you. You got your new dad, Benny, who loves you."

He cleared his throat. "Well, about my job. I didn't tell you the whole truth. Don't fucking lose it."

I swallowed and sat up straight, waiting.

"Soooo, I got suspended for a couple of weeks."

"What? Suspended? Why?"

"Man, it's a long story. I just kinda blew my top a few times. Cursed a few people out. I left a gig early 'cause they kept fucking shit up—stupid shit like that. I was stressed out, man. I got written up, and shit, and well, the suspension was the last warning."

"Oh, man, sorry to hear that."

"Man, they not letting go of me. We good. I already called HR, and I qualify for wellness days. The counselor here told me they got a twenty-eight-day detox program."

"And?" I leaned in.

"Whatchu think? I'm no dummy. A month off?" He laughed, "I'm gonna do it, and I will get my wellness on." He chuckled. "You getting any vibes on this?"

"First of all, I'm upset with you for lying. You could have told me."

"Well, I didn't want to hear that fatherly Mister Perfect tone of voice that you just did."

"Yeah, we'll talk about drugs another time." I felt my jaws clenching. I wanted him to get better, and I figured a lecture wouldn't help him anyhow.

"I'm thinking about working two weeks a month for them anyhow. More like a freelance gig."

I took a deep breath and just listened.

"My business is picking up, so I might not go back full time."

"Noooo, you need to stay with the magazine. Time off in rehab will do you good. You'll get a clear head. You can get more than ten articles done. Don't cop out now. You need this job for your career."

"Is that your spirit guides telling you that?"

"Yes, you need this job. You are just getting started. Don't get cocky and have it all come crashing down on you."

Chapter 16

Kylie

My alarm went off, and five minutes later, I heard a knock on the door. I dragged myself out of bed and yelled, "Who is it?" I looked through the peephole and saw a handsome man in a navy-blue uniform shirt. Chiseled features. Clean-shaven.

"Good morning. Are you Miss Alexander?" He raised his beautiful thick eyebrows.

I cracked the door. Jeez, what a nice one to wake up to. I stood up straighter and smiled.

"Well, gooood morning. I'm the handyman that was requested." His eyes sparkled, and he looked at my baby-tee that read in bright blue letters, *"Happy to Be Nappy"* across my perky breasts. Shit, I forgot to put on a bra. I quickly folded my arms across my chest.

Mr. Handyman-So-Fine said, "Did I wake you?" His eyes went to the satin scarf on my head.

"No, no, I was about to get dressed for work anyhow. I was not expecting anyone." I opened the door more. "What are you here to fix? I'm leaving in an hour."

"Well, as I understand it, some wiring is off in the garage. It was mentioned to our dispatcher. It shouldn't take me long to check it out."

"Oh yeah, the garage door. I do remember her saying it was acting wonky. It shuts when it wants to. You have to hit the button like four times or something. That's why she parks outside most of the time. I don't go in there."

"May I come in and have a look-see?" He had the sweetest voice and had the nerve to have an accent on top of all them good looks. He kinda sounded like Trevor Noah from *The Daily Show*. That South African, British-type accent.

"Sure, you can come in, but what's the name of your company, so I can call her and let her know you're here. She musta forgot to tell me."

"Hmmm, what time will she be back?"

"Not until 1:00 p.m."

"Ah, well, yes, she must have forgotten to tell you, since she booked it for the 8:00 a.m. to 10:00 a.m. window." He adjusted his backpack on his shoulder. "I have a pretty tight schedule today, which is why I'm so early. Not sure I can get back here at 1:00 p.m. Do you mind if I take a quick look?" His eyes floated to my navel that was exposed.

I opened the door and waved him inside. "So, where are you from?"

"Oh, everywhere," he laughed. "My parents moved around a lot, so I have a mixed stew of a lot of cultures. I sound like I have multiple personalities at times."

"You sound British, but then you sound South African, and then like something else. Not sure."

"Yep, I've lived there too."

"Wow, that's pretty cool. Can you give me one minute?"

He nodded. I gently closed the door and left him by the kitchen. I rushed back into the bedroom and took off my scarf. I fluffed up my 'fro and threw on one of Breeze's old sweatshirts, so I wouldn't keep giving him a peep show. My boobs seemed turned on by his smooth voice, or maybe it was just the A/C. When I came out of the room, he was already in the living room looking over an open notebook with Mackenzie's handwriting. He ran his fingers slowly over the notebook. When he caught me looking at him, he said, "Studying to be a doctor?" He pointed to one of her medical books.

"Boy, you sure do make yourself at home quick, huh? And, noooo, not me. That is my roommate, Mackenzie. Miss Alexander."

"Oh, my apologies. I did not mean to be intrusive. But that's impressive. She writes so hard. So intense. Like she's fighting with the paper."

I laughed, "That's her. Intense."

"She must be a smart girl."

"Yes, she's very cool." I led him to the garage.

"How long have you known her?"

Man, he was pretty inquisitive.

"About a month or so. Don't you need your tools?" I pointed to his knapsack he left on the chair in the living room.

"No, I just want to see what's wrong first. It might be a simple fix. I can go to the van if I need more." He slowly walked around the garage, observing the door. He seemed very impressed with the organization.

"This, by far, is one of the neatest garages I have ever seen."

"Yeah, she's a little OCD."

"I like OCD. Makes my life easy. You should see some people's garages. Savages, I tell you." He shook his head.

"I can only imagine the hoarders that are out there."

"Exactly."

I had probably only been in the garage about two times. He opened and closed the door with the switch to troubleshoot it. It was getting stuck just as he thought. While he fiddled with it, I noticed in the far-left corner a golden trophy sticking out of a cardboard box. It was marked *Awards* in a red marker. My curiosity got the best of me, so I opened it. It was a box with over ten Girl Basketball trophies. Wow! They were for various tournaments: first prize and MVP awards. I had no idea she played ball. I would have never guessed that. She had the height for it, though.

What took me by surprise was the name on the trophies. It read *"Sage McKenzie,"* not "Mackenzie Alexander." That was beyond weird. Maybe that was her baller nickname? I had a knot in my stomach. It didn't feel right at all. Who the fuck is Sage? Goose bumps formed on my arms. Then I put the trophy back in the box. I started to pretend like I was organizing boxes to see if I saw anything else interesting, but all the other boxes were taped closed.

"Now, I'll need my bag." He did a light jog back into the living room to get his knapsack.

Mr. Handyman-So-Fine took a few more minutes and then smiled. "All done. There was a short in the cable. I fixed it with some electrical tape. It will cost more to get the electrician out here." He pressed the garage door button to show me it was working correctly.

"Wow, you're fast. Thank you. I'm sure she'll be happy."

"Are you okay over there?"

"Yeah, why?"

"You look a little shaken up."

"No, no, I'm good. Just a lot on my mind. Does Mackenzie have an account with you all? I don't have any cash to pay you."

He gently put his hand on my shoulder. "Oh, no worries. This one's on the house. Just make sure you tell her Mr. Fix It Now was here, and we want to thank her for all of her years of being a great customer." His charming smile shined.

"Oh, thank you . . . What's your name?"

"Warrington."

"Oh, I will definitely tell her. That was so nice of you." I was secretly hoping he'd ask me for my number.

"You have a good day, Kylie." He winked, then raced to his navy-blue minivan with tinted windows.

"You toooo." I waved as he drove away.

Wait . . . Did I tell him my name? I took a big gulp to push down the lump in my throat. I know for sure I did *not* tell him my name. I locked the door and ran for my cell. I tried to call Mackenzie, but the phone kept going to voicemail. Who the hell was that guy? He seemed almost toooo nice. And the way his eyes were darting around the house . . . He was pretty nosy. I Googled Mr. Fix It Now, and no such company existed in the area. My heart started to race. I called Antonio in a panic.

"Yo, I think I just let a stranger in the house."

"What? What are you talking about?"

"He was a handyman. He seemed okay and knew the garage door was wonky. But Mackenzie didn't say I should be expecting anyone, and he fixed the garage without charging."

"Okay, sounds like a nice guy."

"Too nice. That's the problem. And he knew my *name*. I'm sure I did *not* tell him what it was."

"Ky, how you going to let a man in the house? Come on, you *know* better. He musta been good looking."

"What?" I blushed. I was glad I was talking to Antonio on the phone and not in person. "No, he was okay, but that wasn't the reason. He said stuff he could not have known. He knew about the garage, not working."

"Did you get his license plate?"

"No, I was too shocked. I didn't think fast enough."

"And you want to be a PI?" He scoffed, "You gotta get it together, Kylie. Be on your toes."

Ouch, that hurt. I rolled my eyes. "Look, I was in shock. This is a lot to take in, this man coming up in here knowing my name and shit."

"Well, try contacting Mackenzie and see what she says."

"I did call her. No answer. She usually leaves her cell in her locker. But I left a text because she checks her phone on break. But, wait, there's more." I told Antonio about the trophies in the garage.

"Definitely weird. Look, when she gets back to you, just mention the dude. Don't say anything about finding the trophies and shit yet until you get a feel of what's what. You should do some more digging—anything you can find on both names. How long has she owned the house, etc.? You should not come in to work. Wait for her to get home. I'll cover for you at the office. I'll tell Vince you doing research for me. He's not coming in until later today anyhow."

I grabbed my cell phone and entered "Sage McKenzie" and "basketball" into Google. Why would Mackenzie have someone else's trophies in her garage? The constant wig changes were one thing, but what if Mackenzie isn't who she says she is? As I typed rapidly, trying to find out information, a sinking feeling overcame me. Then *bam!* There was a video from about ten years ago of Mackenzie with her hair in a ponytail. She was being interviewed after a basketball game. What was crazy is that the game was in England and when she spoke, she had a very strong British accent.

Mackenzie was a fucking multiple personality psycho. How the hell can she be so British and be full-on Southern belle too? She mentioned one day that she did live in London for a minute, but never went into detail. I remember seeing her watch BBC, and she explained she preferred it to American news—less dramatic and sensational. But maybe she was just trying to feel at home. She loved her tea, said "cupboard" instead of cabinet, and called candies "sweeties." It was starting to click. But why and how did she have such a strong Southern accent?

I sat at the kitchen counter with my laptop. The digital stove clock blinked the time. It was 1:35 p.m. Suddenly, the door flew open. In a hurried voice, she said, "Hey, Kylie, you home? What were you talking about in the text? What handyman?"

"I'm in the kitchen," I called out. And then I took a deep breath. I was going to have to put on the performance of a lifetime. "The handyman said you booked him for this morning to fix the garage. Mr. Fix It Now was the name of the company."

Mackenzie's eyes widened, and she dropped her bags where she stood. "Did you let him in the house?"

"I did. And he fixed the garage and said he wasn't going to charge you."

She raised her voice and walked up close to me. "Fuck. Fuck. Fuck. You let him in? You *let* him in? What was his name?"

"Warrington. You know him? He knew my name too."

She slowly walked to the living room and sat on the edge of the couch, looking defeated. My heart sped up as I saw the dread come across her face.

"Who is he, Mackenzie?"

"Asshole wants me to know he was here. Fucking asshole. He used his real name and the nickname I used to call him, Mr. Fix It. He was handy with everything. Shit, Kylie." She sighed, and her shoulders dropped in surrender. "Warrington is my ex-husband. I gotta get the hell outta here." She got up and starting pacing in the living room, grabbing her head.

"My fucking little sister Lyneise must have told him where I was. I know it had to be her. She was always falling for his bullshit."

"Is he dangerous? Do we need to call the cops?"

"Noooo, we have to go now. He'll expose me. He'll destroy everything I've worked for, Kylie." She walked up to the living room window and closed the blinds. "Did you watch him when he was here? He could have bugged the house. Was he anywhere else in here besides the garage?" She was clearly in a panic.

"He was in the living room, and he looked at your books and asked me about you being a doctor."

"His nosy ass. I gotta get outta here to figure out my next steps. I gotta think. I *can't believe he found me.*"

"This doesn't make any sense." I grabbed her hands to calm her down. "Girl, you gotta tell me what's going on for real so that I can help you. I can call Antonio to come here, so you feel safe. He has a gun, well, if we need one."

"Sheeeeit, I have a gun. Kylie, I really didn't want to bring you in on this, but if he knew your name, he must have been following us. Watching us. Let's go, and I'll explain everything. I don't want to be here for another minute. Come with me."

Chapter 17

Kylie

The afternoon sun beat down on us as we looked both ways to see if Warrington was outside. We were on high alert. My adrenaline was pumping as we hopped in her car and sped off.

"Where are we gonna go?"

"I don't know—just away from here." She was doing sixty in a thirty lane.

"All right, but *chill*." I pointed to the speedometer. "Cops are over here heavy in Coral Gables. Drive to my office. Head to Coconut Grove. I'm gonna text Antonio to meet us."

"Okaaaay. Okay, that's a good idea. What I'm about to tell you, you can't tell anyone. I mean, anyone. He is dangerous, Kylie. He destroyed my life . . . who I used to be. He used to beat me. Beat me so badly. I had headaches. I had constant pain. I would put up with it only because I knew he had a mental illness. I was trying to save him like a dumb ass, and I . . . Well, I was no angel." She shrugged.

"No one deserves to be abused. It doesn't matter what you did or didn't do."

We got to my office and sat down in the receptionist area on the couches. I checked my phone. "Antonio said he'd be here in twenty minutes."

Mackenzie started to talk almost as if she were talking to herself. She seemed dazed in a memory. "I wasn't myself when I was with him. Always walking on eggshells. And I looked for the love I wasn't getting at home." She paused and looked at me. "Kylie, I didn't just cheat. It was with Andre, an ex from high school that Warrington despised because he knew we had a strong love for each other even though years had passed. I got sloppy and didn't realize he was following me, checking my phone, and eventually, he found out everything. I was even pregnant at one point, and I had no idea which one of them was the father."

"Oh my Gaaaawd."

She spoke softer. "Warrington found the pregnancy test in my purse. Our sex life had been nonexistent for some time. He said, 'Who are you fucking? Andre?' I was terrified because I had no idea he knew. Then he smacked me, and I backed away from him, and he kept coming toward me. He smashed me against the wall and kept punching me in my stomach. I cried out for help, but no one came. I know someone must have heard me in our flat, but no one came. It was the scariest moment in my life! He socked me so hard in my face that was the last thing I remember."

I yelled, "Oh, Mackenziiiiie. That is so scary."

"I was in ICU in a coma. They said he left me for dead. He could have killed me. I woke up in the hospital two weeks later with a concussion and many more problems. I should not have cheated. He'd choked me before. He'd punched me before. I knew how jealous he was. It was my fault that he tried to kill me that time."

I felt sorry for her since she was rationalizing abuse. "It was *not* your fault. No man should put his hands on a woman, Mackenzie."

"His jealousy was cute in the beginning, but after a while, he started to feel like my father or a warden. I should have seen the signs from when we were dating, but silly me just thought we were madly in love."

"But was it just a pregnancy test that tipped him off about the affair?"

"No, no. I found out later from my sister that Andre's wife saw our messages and sent screen shots to him. He saw pages and pages of our conversations. Photos and videos he promised to delete. And would you believe, after Andre's wife saw all of this, she *stayed* with him. Andre hasn't contacted me since, even after he learned what happened to me."

"Oh, man, that's horrible."

"I lost the baby, of course. And, well, Kylie, the worst part of the story is that I woke up another person."

"What do you mean, like amnesia?"

"Like a whole 'nother person, chile."

The keys in the door jingled, and Antonio walked in. "Hey, sorry it took me so long. You ladies okay? What's going on?"

We brought him up to date.

"Do you know where this fool stays? Should I go look for him and have a little chat." He cracked his knuckles.

"I didn't even know he was in the US. I knew he got out of jail a few months ago, but I thought no one knew I was here except my family. I have not spoken to him in four years."

"Finish what you were saying before Antonio walked in. You said something about being another person." I needed her to admit what I already knew—that she wasn't who she claimed to be.

"If I told you the whole story, you wouldn't believe me."

Antonio leaned up against the wall with his arms folded. "Try us. If you really wanna get rid of this dude, we need the full story."

"Well, he beat me so badly he gave me a concussion, and I woke up speaking like this."

"Speaking like what?"

"Like *this*. With this ridiculous Southern accent. I'm British, Kylie. I'm *British*. I have not heard my voice in years." Her voice was choked with tears. "Four years, to be exact."

I cleared my throat and wrinkled my nose, reaching for a response. "How . . . is that possible?" And all this time, I thought she was a damn good actress or psychopath.

"I have Foreign Language syndrome." She turned to Antonio and stared at my blank face. "See, I told you, you wouldn't believe me."

"You know, I think I've heard about it. I saw a documentary with a French woman who woke up from a surgery speaking Mandarin fluently. And she never knew the language before. That's some wild shit. It was really crazy," said Antonio.

Mackenzie said, "Yes, it occurs mostly after major traumas to the brain and also after some operations. I was in a deep depression for months. I would hardly speak because I was sick of people laughing at me or looking at me like some freak of nature. Some people think I'm still faking it to this day. Like, who the fuck could keep a prank like this going for so long? Doctors couldn't find out what was wrong with me. I was a pincushion for a few months until a neurologist finally diagnosed me with Foreign Language syndrome. They still don't really know what caused it."

Antonio asked, "Were you in the press?"

"Yes, waaaay too much. BBC News did a special on the subject and interviewed three other people and me about it. I never got peace after that. Only 100 people in the world have ever been diagnosed with it. That story was one of the reasons I wanted to leave and start over. I had no privacy. Warrington stole my life. I hate him for it."

I dug deeper. "So, let me wrap my head around this. You never had any family in Dallas?"

"No."

"You never knew how to imitate someone from Texas?"

"No, I'm as British as they come. The crazy part is I still hear my old voice in my head when I'm thinking or when I'm dreaming. I didn't even notice I was speaking differently at first. My family kept asking me why I was talking 'funny.' Moving here was lonely, but also easier for me. It was so much easier to be someone else. I just studied Southern people and fit right in as Mackenzie Alexander."

"Oh, so your real name is Sage."

"Yeeees. How did you know that?"

"The trophies in the garage. That's a pretty name."

"Thanks. Soooo, now you know." She clapped her hands and sat back, looking relieved. "That's everything." She looked at Antonio.

"I figured you were on the run with all them wigs and shit, but it's good to know you're the innocent one and didn't kill someone," I smiled.

She chuckled. "Yes, on the run, but that shit didn't work out too well, did it? That joker still found me."

"I gotta call my sister, Lyneise. I *know* she's the bitch that gave him my info. It's gotta be her. Mommy would never tell. I was so careful."

Antonio put his hand up. "Don't you use that phone to talk or text. Use it for work. He might have a tracker app on your phone where he's intercepting info. He knows too much."

I agreed. "Noooo, definitely don't call her. He still doesn't really know that I'm on to him or that you know. We can set a trap."

"I like your thinking, Kylie," Antonio said.

"Trap?" Mackenzie laughed. "He's too smart. He wanted me to know it was him. He used his real name and his nickname. It's like he's trying to scare me."

"You want to stay at my mom's tonight? We can stay in my old room until you figure out what you want to do."

Antonio sat down in the chair across from us on the couch. "Look, you not gonna run from this punk nigga."

"Let her think. Do you want to press charges?"

"No, no. He's going to make me lose everything. He can expose me as a fraud. He has too much evidence of my life as Sage. He would use it to destroy my reputation. I need to finish school. My dream of becoming a doctor started with all of this madness. I want to learn how to help others who need healing. He's not going to mess my life up again. Can we just get some things from the house tonight? I need to think, and I don't feel safe there right now. I know he's watching us."

"I'll come back with y'all. I'm locked and loaded if he wanna try me."

"Antonio, stop. I doubt we'll need any guns."

She laughed. "Oh, you think not? I wish he *would* try me now. I got Justin with me at all times *Just-In-Case*."

"Y'all wanna go now?"

Mackenzie said, "Yes, please. Thanks, Antonio, you're a doll, baby."

Chapter 18

Kylie

Antonio sat outside in his car while Mackenzie and I went into the house to gather a few of our things. We had just walked into the kitchen when I heard a door shut in the back near her bedroom.

My hand went on Mackenzie's shoulder. "Did you hear that?" I asked softly.

"Yeah, it's just the wind. I think I left my window cracked." Then we both looked at each other.

Footsteps followed . . . and Warrington came out of her bedroom. "Well, helloooo, again, Kylie. And my goodness, Sage. You're as beautiful as ever." He waved a book in his hand.

Mackenzie froze. I screamed and tugged on her to run with me outside to Antonio.

However, she stood firmly like a stone and said sternly, "What the fuck are you doing in my house?"

Warrington's eyes blinked rapidly. "Bloody hell. It's true. You sound like a true American. A Southern belle even. I can't believe it's true." He held her workbook in his hand and started to walk toward her. "I'm here to say sorry. Come, hug me. It's been four long years. I missed you."

I squealed, "Mackenzie, come on," I yelled. She shoved me off.

"I'm not going any-damn-where. *He's* an intruder. *He* broke into *my* house."

I ran to the door and yelled, "Antonio! He's in here! Come here. He's in here." He didn't hear me with music on and windows up. I had to run out to the car and wave him in. When we got back into the house, Mackenzie was standing there with two hands on her .40 pistol pointed at the center of his head. Her stance was strong like she meant business. Warrington's hands were up in the air, shaking.

"Look, let's talk. I'm not here to hurt you, baby. Sage . . . Sage. Listen to me. I'm here to apologize."

"Don't 'baby' me. How did you find me?"

"Your sister gave me your cell phone number. I told her I wanted to call you to apologize. Lyneise didn't mean any harm. She didn't tell me where you lived."

"So, how the fuck did you find me?"

"Look, put the gun down, please. Please." He waved his hands for her to put the gun on the table. "Don't do anything crazy. You don't want to go to jail. It's not fun."

"No, *you* answer my fucking questions. How did you find me?"

"I traced you to Texas, and your new name was in the reverse phone lookup. I did the rest of the research and saw you were here in Florida. It was not that hard."

"Oh, so you stroll in here with your big balls, breaking into my house, sneaking in when I'm not home, scaring Kylie. You stole my life. You took my identity away. Did you think we would just kiss and make up? I should pull the fucking trigger right now. I would not go to jail, either. *You* broke into *my* house. I should kill you right now. You fucking abusive psychopath!" She took a deep breath, and her voice cracked. "What the fuck are you smiling at?"

He let out a little chuckle. "I'm sorry, I just . . . I just can't . . . can't believe it's you talking. It's like someone possessed you. I'm sorry, I just didn't realize you would sound like—"

"Shut up. It's not funny. It's not fuckin' funny. *You* did this to me." Mackenzie was shaking as she pointed the gun.

Antonio said softly behind her, "Mackenzie, give me the gun."

"Who is he? Your new man?"

"No, I'm the nigga about to save your life." Antonio lurched in fast. He rushed Warrington to the ground and repeatedly punched him in the face.

The coffee table turned over. Books flew. Warrington groaned and got up, then staggered backward. He came back swinging and missed each time. When he fell into a painting, Antonio kicked him hard in the stomach. Warrington winced in pain and looked winded and pained from the scuffle. Antonio pulled out some handcuffs from his back pocket and tossed Warrington flat on his stomach to cuff him.

Mackenzie was in a state of shock. She was speechless—numb. Her hands became limp, and I slowly took the gun from her. Tears flowed silently from her eyes. I hugged her. "Don't worry. He's going to jail now for a long time. Hopefully, they'll ship his ass back to the UK."

Antonio stood over Warrington on the floor. He was doubled over in pain with his hands behind his back. "Call 911. Tell them we have an intruder."

I held the gun very carefully and placed it in a kitchen cabinet. "You have a license for that, right?"

Mackenzie nodded.

"Good, we don't need any more issues."

Blood dripped from Warrington's mouth on the floor. He grumbled, "You didn't have to kick me, mate. I would have complied. My hands were in surrender. What are you, a cop?"

"Shut the fuck up. Don't ask me no questions. Any man that puts his hands on a woman needs a daily beat-down. I went easy on your pussy ass. You getting locked up. Breaking and entering is a felony. I'm sure you gonna get stalking charges too." Antonio shook his head. "You's a dumb motherfucker."

I called the cops and brought Mackenzie into my room with me so she could tell the dispatcher what happened. I wanted to make sure we got her on the recording.

We waited for the police to arrive, sitting on the edge of my bed. We were both still shaken up but relieved that Antonio was here.

"Doctors say I may never sound the same. I may never get my voice back." Her voice cracked. "It's not just the accent. It's parts of me. My personality. I feel like a stranger in my own body at times."

"Don't worry. After we get this motherfucker locked up, I think I know who can help you."

Chapter 19

Jacques

I sat by the window, sipping hot ginger tea. My office was freezing again. I noticed since I'm not eating so much meat, I tend to get colder now. I looked out the window at the heavy traffic and then at my clock, which read 5:55 p.m. My new client, Mackenzie, was on her way.

Kylie and Antonio went through quite a crime scene with Mackenzie. It was a chilling event, and even as she told me about the ex-husband, I could pick up vibes of a mentally disturbed individual. Kylie asked if I could give her roommate a reading, and I didn't hesitate to help out.

She was a beautiful girl. Big, big energy—powerful feminine energy that could captivate a room. I remembered I liked her vibe when I read her energy for Kylie before their first meeting. She wore cat-rimmed glasses, jeans, and a flowing yellow top that came off the shoulders. Mackenzie walked slowly and gracefully . . . but then bumped into a chair and dropped her water bottle.

"Sorry, I'm a bit nervous."

"Don't worry. I don't bite."

"Well . . . good." She laughed and sat down across from me.

"What's your full name and age? Kylie told me some of your story. It's fascinating. I know you have two names."

"Oh, she did? Yeah, it's a shocker. Well, my birth name is Sage Alexandria McKenzie, but I go by Mackenzie now. I'm 37."

"So, this condition you have . . . the doctors do not know how you got it?"

"Yes, well, they say it's from an injury to the brain."

I nodded my head. "Yes, but it feels to me much more than that. You're accessing memories from the past. Sort of what happens when people take certain psychedelic drugs. They may tap into a past life, gain a new skill, and in some cases, start speaking in another language. Usually, it's just temporary, but I understand you've had this a few years now?"

"Yes, four long years. And you know what? I believe you. I heard of that being a connection to tapping into the brain. I've done some research and saw some similarities, but it always amazed me that the medical community views those ideas as 'out there' theories. What's really crazy is that I didn't just wake up talking funny. I would know things I didn't know before: how to cook certain things, how to grow plants, and develop holistic remedies. All of these gifts I never knew I had came out at once after my coma. Like they were stored in a little pocket in my brain that suddenly got unlocked.

"I tried to explain this to the doctors, but they acted as if I were making it all up. That was one of the main reasons I joined med school. I have this enormous urge to heal others now. Those jokers were gonna have me doped up on drugs for the rest of my life. I decided to find natural alternatives for my migraines and to keep me calm. I still have PTSD from all of the abuse . . . from my ex." She tapped her leg nervously.

I lit a white candle on the table. Then I wrote her name down and took a deep breath to ground myself.

"Mackenzie, I'll be right back." I smiled and closed my eyes. I tilted my head to the side and instantly felt as if someone were crushing my head. I felt overwhelmed . . . crowded. There was so much going on inside of her. It was like multiple voices trying to get out. A lot of powerful energies swirled like a cyclone in each of her chakras. My throat tightened, which meant she held in a lot of secrets—blocked throat chakra. My guides said softly, *"Take her hand. Feel her to see her soul. It will help you see more."*

With my eyes still shut, I said softly, "Please give me your hands." Her hands were limp and soft and immediately sent a rush throughout my body. A jolt of energy took me somewhere else.

I saw myself as her, standing next to a river. In the water's reflection, I saw that I was a tall, slender, caramel-colored man with freckles across my nose and cheeks and honey-brown eyes. There were at least fifty people lined up by the river near my small home. Many very sickly with canes or lying down while they waited for something . . . Then I saw that they were anxiously waiting for me.

I suddenly knew. "You were a shaman. In Peru. They called you Hombre Mágico—the Magic Man." I felt a jolt of energy. I suddenly wanted to sit even straighter. I felt proud. "You were very powerful—very." I looked at her as she sat with me and smiled.

"Whaaaat?"

"I see people line up to see you daily. Not everyone makes it to you before nightfall. It's a very exhausting job. You gave a lot of yourself. This was in ancient times. Feels like the early 1300s."

"That's a long time ago. I had groupies?"

"Yes, the crowds are very large. You made potions and teas. Mudpacks and spells of various kinds. A lot of healing remedies for the sick."

"That's sorta what I do now."

"Yes." I paused as I saw flashes of the other side of her work. I had to tell her. "Yes, similar, but you had a dark side to your work then." I saw flashes of him having sex with young teen girls who didn't have money to pay for their sick siblings or dying parents. In some cases, even men would perform acts on him for payment. "You often used your power as a healer to take advantage of people and seek pleasure for yourself."

"Wow, that's soooo not me now." She moved her long hair to one side.

"No judgment. It's called evolution. If you didn't have work to do, you wouldn't have come back better in this life. We all have had dark past lives. Believe me. We have to face the contrast before there is growth."

Mackenzie leaned into the table. "Can you ask when the hell this crazy-talk sickness is gonna go away?"

"Okay, I'll ask." I took a long, deep breath.

I was transported to a big boat. It was a riverboat. I heard a lot of laughter and music. Then I saw the numbers 1871 clear as day as if on a billboard in front of me in gold letters. I asked my guides where I was.

"You are on the Mississippi River."

I suddenly felt my body go limp, and I tasted blood. I was dying. The back of my neck started to throb, so I rubbed it. I winced in pain.

"What's wrong? Are you okay, Jacques?"

"Yes, sorry . . . Yes, I'm okay. I just saw and felt something. You are a man again, but now in 1871, on a riverboat. They had live theater and gambling. Lots of gambling. You were wealthy, a man of status. But there was a bad argument."

My guides pulled me into the story as if I were watching a movie to show me what happened before the taste of blood. *I* was in the movie.

You had a hat on and were holding it down so it wouldn't fly away and grabbing your wife with the other hand. *"What did you do with the money I had in the cabin?"*

"You should not spend anymore. One of the servants told me the captain hires expert gamblers to rob people. You are being fooled, Jake. They are tricksters."

"Oh, that's hogwash. Are you going to believe some nigga servant?"

"You're drunk. Please, calm down. You're making a scene."

"No one is even in earshot of us. Where's the money, Priscilla? I neeeed it."

"I hid it. You're drunk. You're not thinking clearly. You already lost enough for today."

"And I can win it all back." Rage built up inside of him, and he grabbed her shoulders and shook her. At first, she seemed unbothered by his outburst.

"Jaaaake, stop it! It's in a safe place."

He yanked her. She screamed as he yelled, *"I'm not going to ask you again. Where's my goddamn money?"*

This time, Priscilla's eyes widened, and she looked afraid. *"In my purse. Please, let me go. People are watching us."*

He let go and pushed her, and the purse went flying into the water when she backed away, trying to get her balance.

"Silly bitch, why would you do that? Why?"

"I did it? You pushed me, you fool!"

"You go get it now!" He started to pick her up to throw her overboard into the cold water, and Priscilla screamed. Her petite body tried to fight him off. She kicked and tried to wiggle out, but his grasp was too strong.

"You know I can't swim. Put me down. I can't swim."

He walked her closer to the edge and looked down and figured it was not too far of a drop. She could make it, he thought.

They slid across the damp deck to the ledge. "Stoooop it. I can't swim. Jaaaake, stoooop!" She fought to get away from his grasp. Her tiny fists pounded into his shoulders. She shrieked, but the music was so loud on the deck below that no one heard her. At least they thought so.

I shared my vision with Mackenzie in detail, and she was in awe of how much came through so fast. "Your name was Jake. You were about to throw your wife overboard. One shot rang out. Someone shot you in the back of your neck to let her down. You went limp and fell. She went down to the ground with you, trying to revive you, tried to stop the blood. Oh God, there is soooo much blood.

"They didn't mean to kill you, but they did. They meant to shoot in the air to scare you. But the bullet ricocheted off of something and hit you."

"What? That was heavy. Oh my God, I was such an asshole."

"Your guides are telling me that Priscilla is Warrington. He was your wife in the past."

"No waaaay. Now, ain't that the pot calling the kettle black? So, what's that—Karma? I was a bitch to him, so he came back to fuck my life up?"

"In this lifetime, was your ex-husband very controlling?"

"Heeeell to the yes. *Very* controlling and jealous."

"Don't you see why? In that life together, he, well, *she* was trying to save you from being a reckless drunk and gambler, and then you go and get yourself shot. So, in this life, it makes sense why he would want to track your every move or be obsessed, spending his time worrying about you. He probably had a serious fear of abandonment. Priscilla blamed herself for your death and lived with tremendous guilt." I took a sip of water. "Many times, we have a lot going in our subconscious and are not sure why we act the way we do, or why we are drawn to a certain type of person. Our souls keep traveling together until we get it right."

"So, you mean to tell me he came back to boss me around to make sure I don't die?" she laughed.

"Noooo, not at all. But think about it. You were a wealthy, powerful, *Southern* man. Maybe that trauma triggered the accent since it was related to a time when you had power. There are lessons, and you need to search for what they are."

"Well, my guardian angels could have done all that high-vibrations shit and sent me messages without changing the way I speak."

I put my hand up to silence her. More visions came in.

"I see him. Your ex now. He is full of guilt and is not mentally stable. He's more of a danger to himself than to you. I'm seeing him pacing around in a circle in a small room."

"Yes, he's in jail. Good for his ass."

"Yeah, he's not well . . . at all."

"He struggled with a lot."

She pointed to her temple, then shrugged like she could care less.

I heard at least three of my spirit guides talking at once. I could not decipher what they were saying. "One second. I'm still getting information." I took a deep breath. A smile came over my face. I felt calm when the message came through so clear. "Your foreign language syndrome will be cured in a year or less. You need to do more work connecting with that life. His name is Jake."

Then I heard a whisper correct me, so I said, "No, Jaaa-cob. Ah, it's Jacob Miller. You might be able to research him on Google. I can't see what he did, but he was good with money. Maybe an investor or entrepreneur of some kind."

"Maybe he can help me grow my healing business."

"Yes, you need more meditation. More stillness. You are going too fast each day. You have to connect with your soul, your higher self. I'm getting you had many lives in the South. Texas and Georgia, as well as Mississippi." I opened up my eyes and sat back. "So, that makes sense why you tapped into that voice. Think of it as a defense mechanism. I think your trauma helped loosen those memory blocks."

"Maybeeee. That's crazy. So, Texas and Georgia too, huh? I know we're running out of time for our session, but next time, I want to dig into those past lives. You are soooo good at this, Jacques."

I bowed playfully.

"No wonder most people from the South are not really sure where I'm from. I used to think all Southerners sounded the same, so I just picked Dallas as my first home. I guess it's just how people assume people from the UK all sound the same. But it's not true. We can tell if you are from Yorkshire versus Wales. Across the British Isles, there is such a variety of accents and dialects."

"Yes, there are so many. Listen, Mackenzie, this is a rare disease, but more things are happening like this daily, so do not think of yourself as weird. Overall, the world is changing. We are raising our consciousness. The veil is being lifted. It's time you work on healing your past. You're adopting this accent since it's probably one of the past lives that needs the most healing. You were pretty abusive then, so I think in this life, you chose to experience what it felt like to be on the *other* end. It sounds crazy, but it's sort of school for our souls."

"Well, shit, I need to graduate already. I'm so glad Kylie told me about you, 'cause these doctors could never explain why I became Southern."

"Yes, most medical doctors don't deal with the esoteric world. However, times are gradually changing. Many holistic doctors are open to things such as this. You can probably cure this within a year, the more you connect with yourself daily."

"Well, Jacques, this helps me soooo much. One year, huh? I love the sound of that. I need to have a little talk with my Mr. Jake and set him straight. He needs to take his ass back to Mississippi in a month if I can help it. I want my voice back." We both laughed.

"You know what? I'm going to recommend a friend of mine. He's a psychotherapist who does past life regressions. That way, you can experience a past life for yourself. His name is Dr. Steven Roth, here in Miami. Very cool dude, and extremely talented."

"I need all the help I can get."

Chapter 20

Kylie

The office was so peaceful. I looked out the window at the drizzle outside from the small kitchen we had in the back. I had enrolled in private investigator online classes and was gearing up to take the Florida State entrance exam in less than three months. I was enjoying a tuna salad while studying. This shit was really happening. I was going to be a certified snoop. I can see my business cards now . . .

Like a Fly on the Wall
Private Detective Agency
Kylie Collins, PI

Vince said he would give me a raise if I got 80 percent or above on the test. I was already on top of things in my online class, and the only one actually working in a PI office. My dream job just fell into my lap. Who knew? One day, I might run my own agency.

Antonio came strolling into the kitchen and poured himself what was probably his third cup of coffee. He was not really a coffee drinker, but he had pulled an all-nighter working. "How's the studying going? You gonna ace that exam or what?"

"I think I will definitely rock it. I've had on-the-job training. I also listen to training videos and study pretty much every night."

"You will get like 85 percent to 90 percent, if not more. You know this shit, Ky. You're pretty sharp."

There was a hard knock on the front door, and Vince yelled, "Come on in."

A high-pitched woman's voice yelled, "Where the fuck is he? Where is heeee?" Antonio put his coffee cup down and ran to the front.

Vince yelled, "Hey, hey, where do you think you're going, miss?"

When she made it halfway down the hall, Rubia met us face-to-face. She looked different in her work clothes. Corporate even in a royal-blue pantsuit and purse on her arm. Her bright red hair was damp from the rain.

"There you are. You bastard!" She pointed at Antonio. "You took pictures of me? You were spying on me, Will? That's not even your real name, either, is it? How dare you! I can sue you."

"Hey, hey. You're trespassing, and you gotta leave, Rubia."

"Leave, leave?" She laughed, "I'm not leaving until you know what you've done. You think you're a fancy private detective, but did you know Angelo is a fucking pedophile? Do you know he cheated on me numerous times? You want to protect him and *help him?* Now, he won't give me money when we get divorced. He fucks little girls—15- and 16-year-old dancers. Girls our *daughter's* age! He's a sicko, and I refused to sleep with him again. I was getting ready to leave him. I was so close."

I stood there in awe. Rubia's face was beet red. Her hands were shaking. She was a nervous wreck, but also an idiot. If she knew that she had a plan to leave, then why go to a place where you had mutual friends? Stupid. That's that invincible mentality.

Antonio sounded calm, but I could tell he was nervous. "Look, I'm sorry. I was just doing my job. Don't take it personally."

She held her chin high. "Your job is ruining people's lives? Oh, isn't this your girlfriend you were fucking? How nice. She works here too?" She pointed to me and smiled. "I almost ate your pussy."

I flinched back as if I had no idea what she meant. Vince was staring at our interaction.

"You looked good, but now I know you're a snake too."

I said, "Look, girl, you need to get out. You are outta control. Do we need to call the cops on—"

"Oh, did you tell your boss that you fuck while on the job?"

Vince tucked in his shirt and walked in closer. "What's going on, Ant? What case is this?"

"She's delusional." I looked at Vince. "First of all, we did not fuck," I said.

Her eyes were protruding. "Oh-oh, they didn't tell you? I know what I saw. His face was all in your pussy. It must taste really good." She had a sinister chuckle. "They were hired by my husband." She knew she hit a nerve and reached out to shake his hand. "I'm Renata Grella, also known as Rubia."

"Wait, is this Angelo Grella's wife?" he said to Antonio. "I thought he didn't want to pay. I don't remember him signing up."

I remember Antonio told me it was off the books. His personal client, he said. Great, now *I'm* a part of this mess?

***

Rubia said, "Oh, so you skim off the top? That's good for you. A spy and a thief?" She said to Vince, "You know my husband used a lot of our savings to pay him? Now, he doesn't want to give me anything in the divorce. I found out when he showed me the photos today. Then, he mentioned the name of this place. He's an idiot. He was pissy drunk and angry. I can get anything out of him when he's drunk. Now, what am I going to do? You guys need to fix this."

"You're going to have to leave, little Miss Loudmouth," Vince said as he grabbed her arm and pointed to the cameras by the entrance to give her a hint.

"You guys need to spy on Angelo fucking little girls. Send *him* to jail. I'm not doing anything wrong. *He* is."

Antonio helped lead her to the door by gently grabbing her other arm. "Yes, please, you gotta go. If you return, or we see you anywhere near here, we'll have you arrested for trespassing, and I doubt Angelo will bail you out."

She snatched her arm back and mumbled, "Fuck you," as she slowly walked out.

I felt horrible. Vince slammed the door. "So, is *this* what we're doing now, Ant?"

Antonio waved his hands. "Noooo, no, it's not like that. He really needed help, and you know, I know him from the gym. He's kinda 'my dude,' so I felt bad for him. I didn't know about all that pedophile shit, though. I told him I would give him a break."

"Yeah, sure. Whatever. I know you are not exclusive to me. What you do on your own time is your own business, but common courtesy is what I expect from you. That's all." Then he pointed his finger at Antonio. "You don't take a potential client and not tell me. All that other shit she said . . ." He grumbled, "I don't even wanna know." Vince looked at me.

"Man, she's fucking insane. Like I would fuck Antonio?" I rolled my eyes. "We just pretended to be on a date. That's all."

"Yeah, Vince, she's tripping. Trust."

"Yeah, just don't let this shit happen again." He walked off with short, hurried steps back to his desk.

My heart sank. I hated feeling like a traitor. I hoped we hadn't permanently lost his trust.

Chapter 21

Jacques

I picked Hicham up from rehab twenty-eight days after he entered. As we drove to Melissa's house, I smiled as I watched him from the corner of my eye. He was himself again: bright eyes, no more dark circles, and he even filled out a bit. They were feeding him well. The afternoon breeze felt good on my face. I enjoyed the view from the MacArthur Causeway as we headed north.

"Yo, you know how many people be in there on some wild shit? I met former cops, doctors, lawyers, and all. One dude I met was a professor, mad cool dude, but got so stressed out with bills and his ex-wife, so he started poppin' mollies and doing coke. He lost everything and started selling his ass to men. What the fuck? I ain't never gonna hit that low. He probably was gay anyhow. You don't just start doing that shit. I don't care how broke you are," Hicham laughed.

"That's crazy. So, how do you feel now that you completed rehab?"

"I'm good. I feel rested. I feel clear. I don't want to go through that shit again, though. That first week was rough. I felt like a prisoner in a mental institution. One girl in the room next to me would cry every night like clockwork. Another was steady cutting herself on a daily. Lots of mental issues. These are grown motherfuckers, not no kids."

"Well, you're weren't exactly acting like you a responsible adult when you landed in there. Don't judge people when you had your own issues."

"Yeah. You're right. I actually liked the therapy sessions. I'm gonna find someone in NYC."

"Wow, I'm glad. Where we are going now is a good start to that."

"Yeah, so explain to me in detail . . . What are we about to do?"

"Melissa is a healer. She can help you stay grounded. She does a few things like reiki, sound healing, and shamanic breathing techniques. She's pretty talented. I'm not really sure what she's going to do to you. She'll read your energy and decide what's needed. It's not like a cookie-cutter type of session. She goes deep."

He leaned back, smiling. "Ah, shit, you sound like you like her. You fuck her?"

"No, noooo. She's a good friend. And a lesbian. She doesn't want me," I snickered.

"Does she have a fat ass, though?"

"Man, focus on getting healed and not always getting into someone's pants. That's part of your problem."

He raised his arms in the air. "What? Pussy is healing." We both laughed.

"Look, just be open. It might feel weird and 'out there,' but she does incredible work."

"Oh boy, here we goooo. The hocus-pocus crew 'bout to work they magic on me. So, you gonna be in the room? Don't leave me in there alone before I end up in another dimension and shit."

"You'll be fine."

They were in the room for about thirty minutes when Melissa called me in. I slowly cracked the door and was hit with a pleasant aroma. The air was clean and fresh. Lemongrass and tea tree oil mist swirled in the air from her diffuser.

I saw Hicham on the massage table with an eye pillow on him. I said softly to Melissa, "What's up?"

"Stand there. You're going to help me."

"Oh, I am?" I felt a chill come over me. There was a presence in the room other than us. Melissa looked at me. I guess she wanted a witness.

She said gently, "Hicham, I'm getting Jacques to assist me in helping remove some of the heaviness and traumas you've collected in your body."

He was groggy. "Okay, do whatever you gotta do." After some healing, he was so relaxed he trusted Melissa and was not worried anymore.

I could tell she didn't want to frighten Hicham, but we both knew. She pointed to exactly where I felt the presence. At the foot of the massage table was a silhouette of a man. I could see it in the corner of my eye, not if I looked straight on. Some psychics like Melissa could see things straight on. I think I still had a lot of fear around seeing things, so I never saw them very clear.

Melissa asked me to join hands with her at the table and mouthed, "I need your help to send him out." She pointed to the window.

"Okay, Jacques and Hicham, we're going to all breathe deeply together. This is teamwork. Hicham, I want you to release any pain, sadness, and regrets as you breathe out. I want you to picture darkness leaving your body."

"Okay," he said softly. It was refreshing to see Hicham so vulnerable.

"Let's begin." As we began to breathe, Melissa had a large selenite crystal that looked almost like an icicle or a wand. She waved it up and down his body. As we breathed, the entity that was attached to Hicham seemed to fade. I've never before seen anything so dark with my eyes wide open. It was a spirit who seemed to want to be near Hicham.

I asked my guides in my mind, *"Who is that?"*

My spirit guide, Edna, replied, *"He was a lost soul. He died in 1971. Drugs, heavy drugs. He clung to Hicham to continue his lifestyle. He had a lot of self-sabotage. His behavior caused him to overdose."*

I jutted my chin in the direction of the window where the stranger was.

Melissa commanded, "Hicham, release it. Let it go."

Hicham started to whine, almost like a child. "Noooo. I don't wanna. I don't wanna." I looked at Melissa in shock.

She shouted, "You must! Release him." She said to the spirit, "You can't stay here anymore. He is not good for you. You must release him. You don't belong here. Go to the light."

Melissa turned to me and said, "Remember how we crossed over your mom?" She squeezed my hand tightly, and I closed my eyes. I saw a radiant white light sweep in and lead him to a door. The door opened, and two spirits in all white ushered him in like they were saving him from this world.

Hicham started softly crying. Then it got louder. I couldn't believe how Melissa opened him so much. He was crying uncontrollably. He muttered in between cries, "I feel freeee. I feel so good. Thank you, thank you."

I opened my eyes, and the room felt so warm. That dark energy was gone.

She said, "Hicham, you had a visitor. There was an entity attached to you."

"Get the fuck outta here. I felt like something got sucked out of me on that last deep breath we took. I feel so light now."

Melissa lit some sage and started to wave it around the room and then around Hicham. "Well, they are attracted to low vibrations. When you do a lot of drugs and drinking, you can attract unwanted spirits in your aura. They feed off of people in that world. He was supposed to cross over many years ago."

I chimed in. "I got 1971."

"Wow, yes, I knew it was the late '60s or '70s. He took a lot of those psychedelic drugs. He searched for vulnerable candidates and seemed to hop around. Hicham was an open vessel. He was weighing down your energy, Hicham . . . You got so depressed. That's why your addictions got so bad. If we didn't release him, you would have been back to square one in a month or less."

"Oh, man, thank you, guys. Thank you. That's some bugged out shit. Y'all like the ghost busters crew. I just had a fucking exorcism and shit. I'm mad tired, though." He was drained and yet, still funny.

Melissa's voice was calm and soothing. "We'll leave you to rest, Hicham, for fifteen minutes or so. Just relax, listen to the music of the ocean waves, and focus on setting your intentions. Focus on how you want to change your life for the better."

We walked out and went into the den where she had floor pillows. They looked like they were from India. They were so beautiful I almost didn't want to sit on them. We sat down across from each other.

"Soooo, did you see that, Jacques?"

"Yes! Yes—it was a man. Very dark and heavy energy."

"I'm so happy I brought you in. I don't think it would have been as easy alone. Hicham really has been struggling for a while. I think that energy was with him for at least a year or more. He was an angry and lost soul."

I asked, "What did you see?"

"I saw a young man in his 20s. I wasn't sure if he died of suicide or drug overdose. But it felt like he didn't go out nicely."

"Did you notice when Hicham was screaming?"

"I don't think that was the spirit. I think Hicham's soul actually wanted him to stay. It's like he has been used to living in that low-vibrational state. I'm getting that was one of many. He's had more. They were attracted to his energy. They wanted to have power over him."

"Thank you. You really may have added twenty years on to his life. I just pray he stays clean."

I felt relieved that Melissa was such an expert at this.

"You really should work with me more, so I can train you. You're so good."

"I need to get a handle on all these past lives I keep seeing first before I add another skill."

She smiled. "One skill enhances the other. It's just practice. I'm discovering so much about my own abilities each day. I think so many of us are gifted, and all we need to do is study and explore. The power of human potential is limitless."

"No question. Sometimes I really do feel like a mutant or X-Men. That's what Kylie calls me." I smiled. "You're right. Everything can be mastered in time, including my new gifts."

Chapter 22

Kylie

Aaaah, shit. It's about to be on and poppin' this week-end. Breeze is in town, and I'm going to get laid lovely. Thank you, Gaaaawd. I have given up on Chauncey's timid ass. He keeps playing games, so I'm going to leave him alone. Olivia might be right. Maybe he got something, and he's scared to give it to me. He probably got back with his ex. I don't have time for games.

I caught Antonio checking me out daily, and I was tempted. But I worried sex with him would destroy my career. Now that Vince had a hint of us fooling around because of Rubia's big-ass mouth, I'm sure he was going to be watching us more closely. I didn't need the drama. I just thought being single was safest for me right now.

Jacques was kind enough to treat me to lunch today to congratulate me on doing so well on the PI exam. He knew Breeze was coming into town tonight, so we got into an in-depth discussion about relationships. During lunch, he gave me a little mini reading that was pretty eye-opening. He saw me married with a kid, but he claimed his spirit guides didn't want to reveal who the father was yet. I think he knew and just didn't want to tell me before I jinxed it.

"Jacques, my job has me really fucked up. I don't know how you deal with it. I mean, you and I deal with cases of betrayal daily. I'd rather stay single at this point. Leave behind the fairy tale of happily ever after where unicorns and fairies dance, and no one cheats. Maybe Breeze can be my Big Mac, and I'll have a few French fries on the side."

Jacques laughed. "You are too much."

"This way, I won't care if he cheats. If we're both free, there's no cheating. No problems. I don't need to know his details, and he doesn't need to know mine. Just no sex without condoms."

"Wow, you seem to have this all planned out. All you need now is a dude who will go along with this master plan of yours."

"I'm just saying. Who wants to keep living a lie? Don't you feel that you know too much at times about people and the lies they tell? Like how can you even believe in love anymore?"

"Yes, I know it's troubling when you know both sides of the story, or if you know how unhappy they are, and then you see their gushing family photos they post on social media."

"It's a big façade. I mean, when I have to dig into someone's inbox daily and see them having full-blown relationships with people other than their spouse—it's soooo crazy to me. They look like Mr. Rogers or freakin' Clair Huxtable on paper, but they are living complete lies. Some for even years at a time. I mean, why bother getting married? I used to think my mom was just bitter, but she might have been right all along. Everyone cheats."

"Look, although there is a lot of infidelities, I do not deny that there is also a lot of love out there. Not every-one cheats, Kylie. There are a lot of very loyal human beings out there."

"Where? Please, show me. I can never go one day without learning about cheating. It's not just my job. I speak to my friends."

"You ever heard of the Law of Attraction?"

"Yeah, yeah, I know." I waved my hands.

"What you focus on expands. Your own fear of commitment is a part of this story."

"Monogamy is not in our DNA, Jacques. It's unnatural. Maybe that's why we fight it so much. I mean . . . Look at you. The perfect guy, close to being a saint, and you had the perfect girl, and even *you* cheated."

He playfully ducked. "Really? You're coming for *me* now?"

I fluffed up my afro nervously. I probably should tone it down. "Hey, I'm just stating the facts. Even you had a weak moment. It just came out wrong."

"Well, with Dee, it was a strong attraction that built up over time. And we did have a past life together."

"So, everyone fucking around has had past lives together? Fuck outta here."

I laughed. "It's very possible. Our souls have traveled together. Look, Kylie, I get where you're coming from. But I still believe in love. We are human, and we make mistakes. It's a part of the process. The journey, if you will."

"Yeah, yeah, I guess. I will never get married. I will just have like a few life partners."

"I don't know what to do with you. You'll be changing your tune when you fall in love. You just haven't met the right one yet. He's coming, you'll see."

"I doubt it."

"You'll seeee."

Later that evening, Breeze booked a nice room at the Ritz Carlton Hotel in Coconut Grove, so we were going to have a nice time. He didn't want to stay in my house since we wouldn't really be alone, and he didn't want my roommate "all up in it," as he said. He's very private.

The office was closed, and he came by after his meetings to check it out. He walked around slowly, looking at the rooms. "Soooo, this is where all the magic happens, suga? A real private detective agency." He looked up at the fifty-inch screen TV by Vince's desk. Then his eyes floated to my desk. He picked up a photo of me, my mom, and Phantom, our cat. I had a picture of the guys from work and me taped up on my cabinet. He noticed my flowers and said, "Wait a minute, now. Who bought you these?"

"Oh, the guys here got them for me for getting a 98 percent on my last exam. They are very supportive."

His jaws tightened. "Wow, that's nice of them. They seem to really love you. But that's not a surprise." He slapped me on the ass.

"Well, I do make their lives easier. They needed a lot of help."

He shrugged. His jealousy was seeping through his pores. I used to find it cute, but now, it was just annoying. He examined my cubicle like he was looking for evidence of him. "What, no photos of me?"

"Oh, come on, no. I don't like people in my business like that." I was still single anyhow. I didn't know why he thought he was my husband all of a sudden. Funny how distance changes things.

"Oh, okay, you all private all of a sudden."

"Breeze, can you please knock it off? You just got here, and I don't want to start arguing. Let's go. It's getting late." I grabbed my purse and keys and locked up the office.

"I saw there was a nice little Chinese spot down the street. They had good reviews. We can go there and the movies after. You ate there before?"

"Yes, we go there for dinner sometimes after work. I'm impressed you did your research in my town."

He jerked his head back. "My town, huh?" He put his arm around me as we walked out of the building, "Darling, don't get it twisted. You still a Brooklyn chick. You got NYC running all through them veins. You not gonna be here forever."

"Yeah, okay." I raised my eyebrows and bit my bottom lip. He really had it all planned out.

As we walked down the busy strip, I noticed Antonio trying on sunglasses at a vendor's booth. We made eye contact, and Breeze immediately tensed up his grip on my hand. I don't think he realized who he was, so he was claiming his territory.

"Heeeey, Kylie." He nodded toward Breeze while Breeze sized up his tall, broad frame and stopped in his tracks.

"Antonio, this is Breeeeze," I said as if he should know all about him. He flashed a fake charming smile and reached out his hand, and they did the traditional pound and chest bump.

"How you doing, man?"

Breeze looked somewhat relieved. "Oh, Antonio, the dude you work with? The detective, right?" He pointed at him. "How you, man? I heard you be having my baby on undercover missions and shit."

"Yeah, you know—we trying to get this paper. She puts in that work. She's a natural. Excellent at her job. Watch your back."

We all laughed, but I knew Breeze's laugh was a nervous one. I actually got chills. Why did Antonio have to smile so damn big? He looked fake, like he was trying too hard with the small talk.

"Where y'all headed? Doing the tourist mall thing?"

"Just a little. We're going to dinner and a movie."

"Yeah, and probably a little bit more." Breeze took my hand.

I could die. What the hell was going on? A pissing contest? Breeze started slowly walking ahead of me, tugging lightly. He might as well have yanked me away. I waved and said, "Okay, see you Monday. Have a nice weekend."

"All right, y'all enjoy." Antonio turned back to the mirror to try on more glasses.

"What the hell was that, Breeze? That was rude." I shoved his shoulder lightly.

"What? I'm hungry. I don't feel like shooting the shit all night with your little work boyfriend. He was shopping anyway."

"Oh, Gaaaawd, here we go. Now, he's my 'work boyfriend'?"

We walked into the restaurant, and the hostess could tell we were not in a happy vibe, but she smiled extra hard.

She looked at Breeze. "Would you like a table for two?"

"Yes, please. A booth, if possible," I chimed in.

The moment we sat down, Breeze got quiet. He was in one of his moods. The silence was overwhelming.

"What's wrong witchuuu?" I said playfully.

"I want you to quit."

"What?" I wrinkled my nose.

"I want you to quit." His tone was flat, and his face was stern.

"Come on, are you fucking serious?"

He was talking with his hands, flying them in the air wildly. "Look, it's dangerous. You got crazy-ass people rolling up on y'all. Who's to say someone from a case they solved years ago won't come and try to hurt you. Someone can be mad and slice your tires. Niggas is crazy out there."

"Why are you even putting that in the atmosphere?" I dusted the air as if I were pushing it away.

"Ky, you don't have to work anymore. If I'm good, you good. Trust me—all these deals I'm working on is gonna have us set for a long while."

"That's really nice, but this is *my* new career. Just like I'm happy for you, it would be nice if you would feel the same. I love it here. Everything is not about what you want. We've been through this already. I wouldn't mind living in both places later down the line, but I am *not* going anywhere. Plus, don't you remember my mom is preggers? I gotta help her when the baby arrives."

He sighed.

"Okay, so what's reeeeally up? You think I don't know you?"

"I did not like that cat. He had a sneaky-ass smirk on his face, like he knew something I didn't. I didn't like his energy."

"Antonio? Oh, please. You are soooo paranoid. All the dirt you've done coming back to haunt you?"

As I said that, I got a flashback of Antonio eating me out and playing with my nipples at the same time. Shit, Breeze was definitely intuitive. However, I continued with the lie. "For the record, Antonio is *just* my coworker. Nothing more, nothing less. Besides, he has a woman."

"Like that makes a difference."

"Yeah, you would know about that life." I took a sip of my water and rolled my eyes.

"Well, he buying you flowers and shit. He wanna tap that ass. What nigga wouldn't?"

"Breeze, he *and* Vince bought the flowers. It's what coworkers do. Please look at the menu and order. I'm not going to go back and forth about this petty stuff." I looked at the time on my cell. "Aaaand, not to mention, the movie starts in one hour so we better order."

"Okay, suga." He looked at the menu, and the tension subsided.

I really was starting to get nervous, because Antonio did look very phony, like he was trying toooo hard to be nice. I knew it was bothering him that I didn't give him a real chance after the "brownie fiasco." I knew Breeze loved me, but I also doubted he would ever be loyal. Quite frankly, having this job is making me wonder if *anyone* can be loyal.

My gaze went from the menu back to Breeze, bringing me back to the present, and I made up my mind. I couldn't be with him as much as I used to want to. I would just keep it as it was and enjoy the ride.

Chapter 23

Kylie

After Breeze's visit, I was clear. I had a good time, but I knew I could not deal with his controlling ways. The next morning, I was just about to get in my car, on my way to work out, when I got a text from the last person I wanted to hear from.

Hicham: Hey, beautiful, I just wanted to thank you. You telling Jacques probably saved my life. I'm sorry for acting out.

Kylie: It's all good.

Hicham: It will never, ever happen again. That's my word. I'm headed back to NY, and I'm clean and sober. I'm gonna get my shit together.

Kylie: I'm glad you're okay.

Hicham: Maybe when I come back, we can try again.

Kylie: Maybe not. Lol

Hicham: It's all good. I hear you. You got jokes, but I hear you.

Kylie: Take care of yourself, Hicham.

Hicham: I will, peace.

Well, that was awkward. I'm kinda glad he didn't call me. It's been more than a month, and I'm still a bit spooked at how he was acting so damn crazy that night he attacked me. I really hoped he cleaned up his act. It would be such a waste of good talent if he just became a drug addict—or worst, if he died of an overdose. He better thank his lucky stars for a big brother like Jacques.

I hopped in my car to head over to my new workout spot. My bestie, Olivia, has been raving about Cultural Expressions, this yoga and dance studio in Hollywood. We were supposed to go together, but then her daughter came down with a fever. But I was ready to have a great time. I'd signed up for a belly dance class and a yoga class. The place was pretty packed, and I was happy to see the owner was an African American woman. You don't see that much here, especially in South Florida.

After two hours of shimmying and hip bumping, followed by deep stretching in a Yin-Yoga class, my body was singing my praises. With all the jogging I do, this was a great workout to get out kinks.

The teacher, tall and elegant, kinda reminded me of a mature Beyoncé. We stood by the receptionist's desk. She nodded her head in approval. "You were very good. I see you got the moves."

"Really? I felt like I had two left feet."

"No, no, you catch on quick."

"I still got it." I raised both hands in the air. "Thanks for letting me know. I was a little nervous."

"Oh, it takes time, but not bad for the first time."

Students started to spill out of the room next to us.

"Hey-Hey, Miss Sophia!" The voice was familiar.

My head turned around fast to match the face with the voice. I smiled at the lovely Latina who had her hair up in a bun and yoga mat under her arm. She looked at me quickly and then pretended as if she didn't recognize me, but I knew she did.

Sophia said, "Wow, Vicky, so nice to see you. I see you signed up for private Belly Dance lessons this week. So, get ready. I'ma take you to the Motherland."

"Oh, I know you will. I need it. Been stressed."

I looked at her and waved. She smiled flatly as if just realizing who I was. "Oh, heeey, Kylie. Are you a member here?"

"Nope, not yet. Today was my first time."

Sophia excused herself to ring up some customers buying incense, and I thought it was perfect timing.

"Listen, Vicky, can I talk to you for a minute outside?" She shrugged reluctantly, acting as if she had to leave. "Look, I know we didn't really get to know each other well, and you had your suspicions about me, but I just want to clear the air."

Vicky tilted her head like she wasn't in the mood to entertain me.

"Jacques told me you thought he and I had something going on more than friendship because of the text I sent him. I just wa—"

"Look, I know what I saw." She put her yoga bag down between her legs. Her hands were crossed, and she widened her stance. "You said, I think I love you. Dedicated a song to him and all. That was cute. It's all good. He's easy to fall in love with. Trust me; I get it. I don't want to keep going over it again. I was more pissed 'cause you were up in our house and smiling in my face."

I raised my voice slightly. "Can you please hear me out? That's just it. You got it all wrong. One night when we were working together, the song came on, and he asked me the name of it. He really liked it, and I even told him it would be nice of him to play it for you, so I sent it to him. That was *it*. I would never cross the line with him. I know how much he loves you. He has been nothing but the perfect gentleman around me, like a brother."

Her eyes softened, and she shrugged. I continued my plea. "Jacques has been miserable without you. He just works out, goes to the gym, eats some fancy vegan shit, and goes home." We both chuckled. "He really is a good dude, Vicky. Give him a second chance. He's not out there like some of these players in Miami."

She uncrossed her arms. "So, he talks to you like that?"

"Yes, we're cool, and he doesn't do much but go to work, so I see him a lot around the office. I know he misses you dearly. It's all over his face. I'm sorry if I'm being too personal, but what are the odds I bump into you all the way up here in Hollywood, nowhere near Coconut Grove? That's a sign."

"Yeah, I know. I almost wasn't sure that was you when I first saw you. I appreciate you for telling me your side, but there was a lot more to the story. We didn't break up just because of you. He did try to explain, but I didn't want to hear it. So, thanks for making me listen. I believe you."

"I *know* it looked bad, but it definitely was not what you thought. You know when shit is read out of context, it can just blow up." I put one hand on her shoulder. "Soooo, we good now?"

"Yes, girl." She opened her arms and hugged me. From what I remember, she was not a hugger, so that was a good sign.

I said, "So what do you think? You gonna give my boy a call? He's all alone now." I raised my eyebrows.

"Well, I got some things to think about first. Please don't mention to him that you saw me yet."

"Okaaaay, mums the word." I zipped up my mouth. "I'm gonna join this spot, so I'm sure I'll see you around in belly dance class or yoga."

"That's perfect. Okay, see you around again. Thank you."

I waved and felt so good as I walked off. Jacques deserved happiness.

Chapter 24

Jacques

A week after rehab, Hicham was ready to head back to New York. As I got out of the car to help him with his bags at the airport, he shocked me with some good news.

"So, I didn't wanna say nothing, but my last week at the center, I asked for only vegetarian meals. I can't do the vegan shit yet, but it's a start."

"That's awesome. I know you love your bacon and steak."

"Yeah, I do. But I was doing a lot of reading up on it, and I think it can help me. Give me some discipline. Help me keep cleansing out my body. And shit, if I can start looking all swole and lean like you, I'm really gonna get a lot more pussy." He rubbed his hands together.

I laughed, "Maaaan, whatever. But I'm proud of you."

"Yeah, well, I know you saved my life, so I gotta work on saving myself. I'm gonna make it up to you, Jay."

"Love you." I hugged him hard.

"Love you, bro." He patted me on the back and took his bags. "I'ma hit you when I touch down."

After dropping Hicham off at the airport, I was feeling confident that, maybe, just maybe, this time, he learned his lesson and was willing to get his life in order. As I walked into my apartment, I smelled a familiar smell. The hairs on the back of my neck rose. It was *her* scent. My heartbeat raced. I did not know if I were hallucinating or if it were wishful thinking. Then as I walked in further, I saw something odd. There were a few silver coins I never saw before sprinkled on the rug. I bent down and picked them up. They were fake. Plastic. Very weird.

Then I heard something jingle in the back room like bells or chimes. I jumped and looked down at the end of the hallway and saw her.

"Vicky. Oh God. What are you doing?" I chuckled nervously. "You look . . . You look incredible." My stomach fluttered. I had to be dreaming. She put her finger up to her lips to tell me to be quiet.

She was dressed as an exotic belly dancer. She was beautiful. I mean *stunning*. She wore elaborate eye makeup and even had a diamond bindi on her forehead. Vicky wore a purple and silver skirt that flowed to her ankles, and a coin belt covered her waist and bottom. As she came closer, I noticed she had on a bra full of gold and silver coins, and her cleavage was so voluptuous.

Vicky's high ponytail was reminiscent of the *I Dream of Jeannie Show*. I loved how she stayed in character and floated toward me, slowly flying the veil behind her. Always the master at role-playing. I was in awe.

She pointed to the couch as to tell me to sit, still not uttering even a word. I did as she commanded and took a seat. My heart was doing flips. I was so nervous. Vicky was back. She was role-playing with me like she used to do. It's as if we never broke up. She walked over to the speakers and pressed *play* on her phone.

The music started with slow and sensual flutes. A woman started singing in Arabic. She teased me with her veil, made slow, sweeping movements with it covering her nose and mouth as she teased me with her eyes. I know I must have had the goofiest smile on my face as I sat back, taking it all in. Suddenly, the music picked up the pace, and she began skipping in a circle and bumping her hips hard and fast to the drum. I started clapping along to the beat. It was such a lively song. I was excited.

"My God, when did you learn all of this?"

Vicky bent down, kissed me, and cracked a smile. She loved my reaction. She danced away and looked back slowly.

"Wait, it's over? Where are you going?" I laughed. I raised my hand like a child in class. "I would like a lap dance, pleeeease."

She made it to the bedroom and shut the door. I figured she had another outfit or something else planned. The music continued to another song of fast-paced drumming. I waited a few more minutes, but she never came back out. I slowly walked down the hall, like a kid about to sneak into a room he shouldn't enter. I was bursting through my pants at this point. The anticipation was too much. When I opened the door, she was standing there . . . naked. Oh, so naked.

"Oh yeeees, that's what I call a grand finale." I hugged her, grabbed her face with both hands, and started kissing her and caressing her body. I pulled away and looked into her eyes. I examined her as if I couldn't believe she was real. That's when I saw her eyes. They were tearing up. I didn't say anything. She started undressing me, and I helped her.

In between quick, passionate kisses, she finally spoke. "I've missed you."

I said in her ear, "I've missed you more." I kept kissing her face and neck. My hands explored her breasts, her hair, her butt as if it were the first time I saw her naked. "This was a nice surprise. I mean really, *really* nice, Vic."

She opened my pants and slid my jeans down to my ankles and started stroking me with her warm hands. I was so hard. I couldn't wait.

"Oh, I missed *him* so much." She moaned as she looked down at my pulsating manhood in her hand.

"Oh, only him?" We both laughed.

"No, you too, Papi, you too." She softly stroked me, and my knees felt weak.

My voice deepened. "Show meeee. Show me how much." She knew what do to turn me into an animal. I was going to give it to her rough, the way she liked it. Vicky bent down on her knees and started to pleasure me. I could hardly hold it together. She started slow and deliberate, and then she got fast and used her hands to jerk me as she sucked. She was making my body sway with pleasure. Vicky was a skilled master of fellatio.

"Oh, maaaan . . . Baaaaby, I missed you soooo much." I grabbed a fist full of her ponytail and pulled her away so I wouldn't come.

She moaned, "Fuck me, Papi. Fuck me."

I bit my bottom lip, looking down at her, begging me to give it to her. I missed her calling me Papi. I picked her up and walked slowly and awkwardly to the bed. I had my jeans still caught around one ankle. I dropped her on the bed, and she laughed. Vicky held herself up by her forearms, smiling at me. Her ponytail came out from me grabbing it. Vicky's untamed hair was scattered across her face. I climbed on top of her and started to suck on her nipples and kiss all over her stomach. I slowly glided up to her neck and let my hardness rub against her. She was going crazy because she wanted me to plunge into her. I was going to make her wait a little bit more. I stuck two fingers inside her. She was so tight. I could tell she wasn't having sex. At least that is what I hoped. I was so happy she was back.

"Stop playing. I want to feel you inside me, Papiiiii."

Our breathing was heavy. The anticipation was rising. "Open those legs for me. Open them." I eased inside her slowly, and she was so moist and warm. I fit like a glove. I felt at home again. We both sighed like we were in ecstasy. I started to get into a groove and began thrusting deeply into her walls, hard and smooth strokes, just how she liked it. She screamed as if I were hurting her, so I stopped and looked down to check her. "Are you all right?"

She slapped my back hard. "Don't stop. Keep going. You are right there. I missed this diiiick. Aye, Papi. Don't stoooop."

I stroked her deeply, and I felt all of these waves of emotions come over me. I looked into her eyes and saw her tearing up again. I saw another face this time. I shook my head because I didn't want a vision. Not now. Not now, I told my guides. It seemed to work.

She panted, "I love you. I love yoooou."

"I love you too, baby." I planted kisses on her neck and face. "Don't ever leave me again."

"I won't." At that moment, she sighed so loud. "Right there. Oh shit, baaaaby."

I couldn't hold it anymore. I collapsed on top of her after I came, and we just giggled like silly teenagers. "I'm sorry," I said in her ear.

"No . . . No, that was so gooood. Amazing." She turned to me and wrapped her legs into mine. She stared for a minute at me in silence. Then she said softly, "I saw Kylie. She explained to me about her text. I'm sorry I didn't listen to you."

"You did? Wow. When?"

"Belly Dance class a couple of days ago. I was hoping the key to the house still worked." She ran her hands through my waves and snuggled on me more.

"I told you, I wasn't going to change it. I was patient."

"And I have a confession." I tilted my forehead into hers. "There was no one else." My eyes widened. "Really? So, you weren't seeing anyone?"

"I went on one date, but I hated the way he chewed, and he was so boring."

"Really, Vic? The way he *chewed?*"

"Yeah, it's the little things that can irk your nerves."

"Well, lucky for me he chewed like a horse." We laughed. "Soooo . . . Are you back for good?" I tapped her chin and kissed her.

"I was going crazy at my sister's."

"Oh, seeee, that's the only reason you returned?" I raised one eyebrow. My hand caressed her collarbone and her chin. She inched in closer to me.

"No, no. You *know* I missed you." She sighed. "I missed us."

"Let's make us a little bit more permanent. Are you ready for this?"

"Yes, I wanna come home." We kissed.

"I want you home and . . . I . . . I want you to be my wife, Victoria Moreno." I can't believe what I just said, but somehow, I knew it was all going to work out. It felt right.

She gasped. She nodded her head yes and started crying. I moved her hair out of the way, and she kissed me, smiling.

How I missed seeing her smile. I was going to enjoy a lifetime of making it all up to her.

The End